The
EVER
NEVER
HANDBOOK

SOMAN CHAINANI

THE SCHOOL for GOOD AND EVIL

The EVER NEVER HANDBOOK

with
AMI BOGHANI

Illustrations by
MICHAEL BLANK

HARPER
An Imprint of HarperCollinsPublishers

IN THE FOREST PRIMEVAL

A SCHOOL FOR GOOD AND EVIL

TWO TOWERS LIKE TWIN HEADS

ONE FOR THE PURE

ONE FOR THE WICKED

TRY TO ESCAPE YOU'LL ALWAYS FAIL

THE ONLY WAY OUT IS

THROUGH A FAIRY TALE

CONTENTS

Student Life

The Graduating Class

Admissions

Frequently Asked Questions

WARNING:
DON'T BELIEVE EVERYTHING YOU READ!

The book in your hands claims to be an official "handbook" to the School for Good and Evil, with "everything you need to know" to graduate a future hero or villain. It says so right there on the inside cover.

But as you'll soon learn, what you see isn't always what you get. And if you don't know what this school is really like, well, you won't just end up an enchanted toad or beanstalk . . . you could end up dead.

Lucky for you, I noticed a stray handbook in the Supper Hall when I came back to visit and have been secretly adding my own thoughts so that whoever finds it will know the truth about this place. Even though I might be a proud graduate of Evil, I knew that if I could help even one of you—Ever or Never—then I'd have done my duty as a survivor of this school. After all it was only because of my friends that I lived to write these very words.

And seeing how you have no friends here yet . . . well, you'll just have to rely on me, won't you?

HESTER

Dear Nevers,

It was only three years ago that I stood where each of you does now: about to start my first year as a student of the School for Evil.

But Evil was different then. The word itself invoked ugliness, misery, and poor hygiene. Evil wasn't just on the losing side of every fairy tale the Storian chose to write; Evil *acted* like losers.

In such hopeless times, it takes a ferocious leader to turn the tide—a leader with vision and persistence. A leader with guts. A leader like *me*.

This isn't your grandmother's School for Evil. The uniforms are new. The classes are new. Even the castle is new (or as new as an obscenely old castle can be). Because our brand of Evil is new! Good may not approve of our fresh face, but do not pay the slightest attention to such fusty thinking, meant to keep Evil in a dark and gloomy supporting role. With me at the helm, we shall bring Evil into the spotlight and celebrate our youth, mystery, and cutting-edge allure.

For what is Evil at its core but a rebellion against Good?
And in these times, Good has become stagnant and boring.
It's Evil's time now, and together we'll rebel with flair.

And if we manage to bring a few Evers into our ranks along
the way, we'll be sure to make room. After all, with Good so
old and obsolete . . . who can blame them?

Sincerely,

Dean Sophie

Sophie of Woods Beyond
Dean of Evil

My Dearest Evers,

Welcome to your new home!

Every four years we invite the best of Good, whom I, as Dean, am entrusted to teach. From Rapunzel to Tom Thumb to Snow White, many of the greatest heroes have graced these halls before they found their way into eternal legend.

It is common knowledge, of course, that Good always wins in fairy tales. For the past several centuries, Good has vanquished Evil at every turn, no matter how nefarious the threat. And yet, our streak of victories had left us complacent, I am sorry to say. Indeed, if it hadn't been for the arrival of a student named Agatha in our previous class—now Agatha of Camelot, of course—we may have continued our descent from a Golden Age of Good into an Age of the Inconsequential. Agatha helped remind us all that Goodness is an open heart, even in the face of the greatest Evil. Indeed, it wasn't so long ago that I called the Dean of Evil *my* own best friend.

But Evil is under a *new* regime now and one that appears to play by a different set of rules. Be respectful, be welcoming . . . but be wary. They are still the enemy, probing our weaknesses like snakes in the sand.

But you are Evers through and through, my children. And as long as you honor the truth of Good's cause, then it is only a matter of time before Evil retreats to its shadows, beaten and humbled, as it has every year before.

Warmly,

Clarissa Dovey
Dean of Good

TO Dean Sophie
   Mischief Tower
   The School for Evil

Enclosed please find a drawing of your proposed changes to the School for Evil, per our meeting last month. We here at the Everwood Architecture Society are thrilled to be working on such an exciting project; this is the most ambitious design we have undertaken since completing Captain Hook's bachelor pad aboard the Jolly Roger.

Of course, a two-dimensional image cannot fully convey the true glory of what this building will look like once complete. Allow me to walk you through each of the new features and explain how they fit into your spectacular and courageous vision.

1) **STYMPH LANDING PAD**: New Nevers will no longer be dumped into the "stinky moat" upon arrival at school. Instead, Evil students will enjoy a pleasant landing on this polished marble ledge attached to Vice Tower—a much more civilized introduction to their new home!

2) **REVOLVING SUPPER HALL:** *The next generation of dining facilities offers 360-degree views of the Endless Woods.*

   (*Note: We will need to hire experts from the White Rabbit's Clock-Making Factory to assist us in constructing oversize cogs and gears.)

3) **DEAN SOPHIE'S QUARTERS:** *As requested, the School Master's tower will be converted into your own private residence. The top floor will serve as a walk-in closet, with separate sections for shoes, cloaks, gowns, and tiaras, as well as a built-in vanity station and hair salon. The second and third floors will house living quarters, with all walls and ceilings made entirely of mirrors. The bottom floor will contain a vast dining facility for dinner parties. The walls of the dining room will be decorated with portraits of you, Dean Sophie, from throughout your life.*

4) **SOPHIE'S WAY:** *We understand that every minute in the Evil Dean's busy day is priceless! This bridge connecting your private tower to your office in the School for Evil will make your daily walk to work effortless and brief. We have budgeted for rare enchantments in order to keep students and uninvited faculty from crossing over.*

5) **EVIL GROOM ROOM:** *Per your request, "Evil doesn't have to be Ugly" will be engraved on the doors.*

6) **EVIL HALL:** *We referred to your notes from the "1ST Annual Villains No Ball" to imagine the new and improved Evil Hall. Black diamond chandeliers will dangle from the night-sky ceiling; the stained glass windows will depict your greatest triumphs against Good.*

7) **TUBEWAYS TO THE BEACH**: *In addition to making intercastle transport a snap, the tunnels are lined with enchanted glitter that sprinkles on the students as they pass. If a student has permission to leave school grounds, he or she will arrive at his or her destination all sparkly and ready to party! However, if the student does not have permission to leave school grounds, the glitter will create a rather vile and uncomfortable case of blood blisters once it touches skin.*

8) **JUICERY**: *In order to comply with your updated Evil Meal Plan, the Juicery has built-in taps that serve liquefied concoctions containing cucumber, beet, and carrot for the improvement of complexion and reduction of flatulence.*

9) **DOOM ROOM NIGHTCLUB**: *Every Saturday night, the Doom Room will turn into an exclusive nightclub, only for Evil students with high rankings and your personal guests. It is my understanding that crogs make very good bouncers, so I suggest you employ one to keep Evers out.*

10) **SOPHIE'S BEACH**: *Hardworking faculty members who need to rest their weary feet can now do so in a private cabana. We have included a cabana-wolf service station for moat-side meal service.*

11) **WINNERS' WEATHERVANE**: *A statue of your gracious self, made from pure Bloodbrook onyx, tops the remodeled School Master's tower. Your finger points at whichever school is currently winning the newly announced Annual Challenge Competition between Good and Evil.*

We hope that this design is to your liking. Please be aware that we project a timetable of seven years to complete construction and that the last-minute changes you sent over have considerably raised the building costs.

Please feel free to contact us with any questions.

Sincerely yours,

Rena Rotunda

Rena Rotunda, Licensed Architect
Everwood Architecture Society

P.S. Just as we were about to send this letter, we received a surprising communiqué from one Dean Clarissa Dovey. We feel obligated to inform you of her statement that these renovations are "not now nor will ever be" approved by the Board of Directors of the School for Good and Evil. She went on to say, and I quote, "Our school is based in tradition. No Dean, now or ever, will be allowed to turn it into an amusement park."

P.P.S. We were confused by your written request to "make Tedros look fat" in all renderings. King Tedros of Camelot is a trusted client, and, with all due respect, we can assure you that he is as svelte as ever.

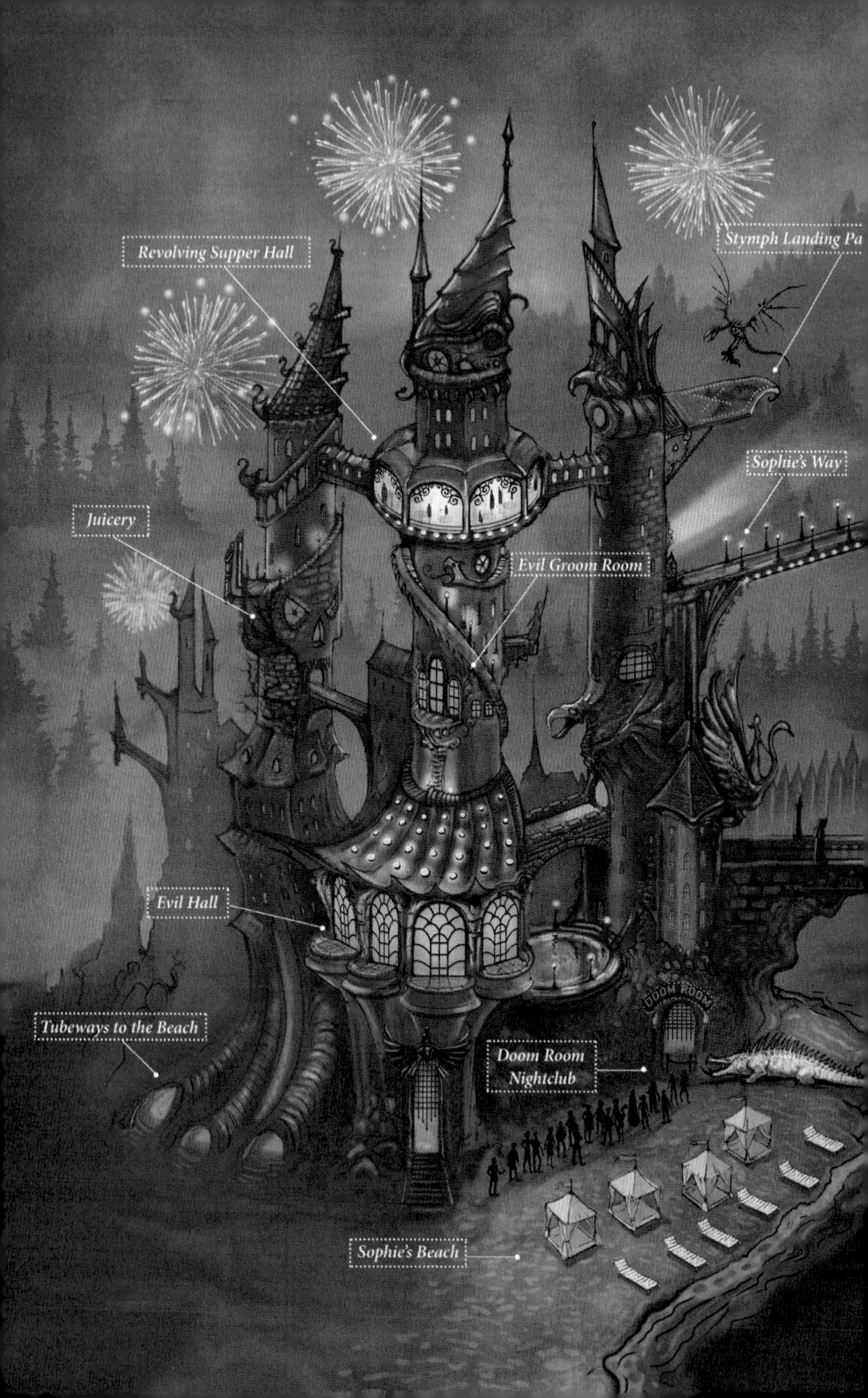
Revolving Supper Hall
Stymph Landing Pa
Sophie's Way
Juicery
Evil Groom Room
Evil Hall
DOOM ROOM
Tubeways to the Beach
Doom Room Nightclub
Sophie's Beach

Winners' Weatherwane

Dean Sophie's Quarters

A New Vision of Evil

School Supplies

The School for Good

EVERS SUPPLY LIST

DEAN'S NOTES:

❋ Uniforms, books, and schedules will be provided upon arrival.

❋ Due to our new mission of gender equality, the following list applies to both Everboys and Evergirls.

REQUIRED:

1 trunk made of Gillikin mahogany with the student's initials engraved

1 Flowerground Pass (included in Admissions Package)

4 boxes of crisp parchment (no crinkled sheets, please!)

14 peacock-feather quills

1 beaver-tooth quill sharpener

4 bottles of willow-sap ink

STRONGLY RECOMMENDED:

1 Briar Rose® sleep mask, set for 8 hours a night

2 cumulus-nimbus pillows with dewdrop embroidery

1 silken-moss bedspread

- 10 pairs of anti-callus alpaca kneesocks

- 1 moleskin yoga mat, with sweat-minimizing enchantment

- 1 self-affirming magic mirror, set on level "Blind to All Flaws"

OPTIONAL:

- 1 pack of Hinderpöllen pills (for those with allergies to plants)

- 1 pair of whisper slippers for late-night trips to the toilet

Due to an alarming lack of discipline in the School for Evil, pranking in Ever dorms has become a very real concern. The following items are recommended for all new Ever students in order to counteract these pranks:

- 1 flutterflea-resistant mattress cover

- 1 set of impenetrable lambswool curtains

- 1 bottle of skunk-scent neutralizing tonic

- 1 personalized, life-size wooden decoy (Geppetto's Workshop makes the most convincing ones)

- 1 pair of clippers with cobra-tooth blades (NOT the python-tooth model; they won't cut through enchanted vines)

The School for Evil

NEVERS SUPPLY LIST

DEAN'S NOTES:

※ Uniforms, books, and schedules will be provided upon arrival.

※ Despite the SGE's new mission of gender equality, boys and girls have different beauty needs, as Dean Sophie knows from personal experience.

REQUIRED FOR ALL STUDENTS:

1 trunk made of Ooty-Kingdom black coral with the student's initials emblazoned in gold leaf

1 stymph-ride pass (included in Admissions Package)

4 sheaves of smooth birch-bark scrolls (parchment can cause paper cuts, which are *so* unsightly)

14 raven-feather quills

1 piranha-jaw quill sharpener

4 bottles of shark-blood ink

REQUIRED EXTRAS FOR NEVERGIRLS:

17 snakeskin pouches of honeycream for daytime use

17 snakeskin pouches of hollyoak
    serum for overnight moisturizing

1   platypus-bill hair straightener

1   pair of crow-beak hair-braiding tongs

1   pair of cuticle-reducing bullhide gloves

REQUIRED EXTRAS FOR NEVERBOYS:

1   stingray-tail straight razor

1   jar of shaving jelly

1   pair of barbell boulders

STRONGLY RECOMMENDED:

1   Evil Fairy® sleep-inducing spindle,
    set for 8 hours a night

2   storm cloud pillows with hailstone embroidery

1   poisonous hemlock bedspread

1   self-denigrating magic mirror, set to level
    "No Pain, No Gain"

OPTIONAL:

2   packs of Hindersunshine pills (for those with
    allergies to bright light and/or good behavior)

1   pair of enchanted sleep shorts with an
    extra-strength night-fart filter

MY SECRET SUPPLY LIST

BY HESTER

Official supplies will only get you so far. If you want that extra edge at the School for Good and Evil, here's what you really need. (You too, Evers—you're not too Good to play a prank.)

3 BAGS OF INSTA-GRUEL (my preferred flavors: Toadstool, Cream of Booger, and Wild Leech); will come in handy for midnight snacks and secret journeys into the Woods

1 CLAW-SHAPED CANDLE for your night table, available at Scents & Sensibility (shop locations throughout the Endless Woods); helpful for doing mischief after curfew in both the Good and the Evil dormitories

4 BOTTLES OF INVISIBLE INK; important for writing down secret spells, protecting diary entries, and passing notes to allies during class

1 GARLIC MEDALLION, for warding off any Evers who get too close

1 DAINTY DAFFODIL CHARM BRACELET. for warding off any Nevers who get too close

3 "EXTRA-PUTRID" STINK BOMBS (available by mail order from Jesters's Jinx Shop); effective for clearing large areas during Forest challenges or when you just need alone time

1 BOX OF DEATHLY-TEA LEAVES OR **1** DECK OF TAROT CARDS OF DOOM, both of which predict brutal deaths with every reading; useful for unnerving rivals before the Trial by Tale

1 PACK OF LIZARD-TAIL BONES. for picking locks

1 CARTON OF VOICE-LOSS LOZENGES. for dealing with over—talkative roommates and avoiding oral examinations in class

1 MAMMOTH-SKIN DRUM, to accompany evil jigs; use for shaming your rivals after they've been beaten

1 TUB OF WANDA THE WITCH'S WART-GROWING SALVE, in case your skin becomes too smooth

1 SET OF CROG-BONE WIND CHIMES; hang them on your door to thwart any murderous intruders

School Uniforms

School
PRE−SCHOO

EVERGIRL UNIFORM:
→ DRESS: Apple-blossom brocade; pearl embellishments from the Nymph Oyster Nursery
→ SHOES: Enchanted dancing slippers (can also increase running speed in case of Banshee attack)
→ ACCESSORIES: Pegasus-feather headdress and fan

EVERBOY UNIFORM:
→ COAT: Jacquard dinner jacket; gold buttons from Midas' Court
→ BREECHES: Slender-fit minotaur wool in amethyst
→ CRAVAT & STOCKINGS: Hand-stitched whisper silk
→ WIG: Woven from pure Altazarra unicorn hair
→ SWORD: Only to be used for official school portraits or to fend off a Harpy invasion

*HISTORICAL NOTE: *In its early years, the School for Good and Evil lacked both a strong School Master and a dedicated Blue Forest. Consequently, creatures from the Endless Woods periodically trespassed onto school grounds and attacked students, with often-lethal*

NEVERGIRL UNIFORM:

→ COAT: Tigris-fur cloak; copper
embossment from Smee's Booty Auction
→ COLLAR: Shadow-silk ribbon
→ SHOES: Blade-tipped slippers, sharp
enough to poke out a cyclops eye
→ ACCESSORIES: Defanged hydra

NEVERBOY UNIFORM:

→ COAT: Embroidered cobra-skin
overcoat with carbuncle buckles
→ PANTALOONS: Wide-fit chintz in
bubonic black
→ SHOES: Sharp spade loafers, helpful
to dig trenches in sudden battles
→ KNIFE: Recommended for defense
against rogue stymphs in the Woods, but
FORBIDDEN in the castle at all times

results. In addition to being impeccably dressed, then, students had to be ready to defend
themselves and others at all times.

EVERGIRL UNIFORM:

- → DRESS: Tea-length chiffon in raspberry soufflé
  (by Cinderella's Mice Designs, Ltd.)
- → SHOES: Blush-satin Mary Janes (Each girl receives
  one pair—no exception for slippers left at the ball!)
- → ACCESSORIES: Rose diamonds with
  fairy-dust polish

EVERBOY UNIFORM:

- → COAT: Cornflower blue embroidered with
  antique Rumpelstiltskin gold straw
- → BREECHES: Slender-fit starched linen
  in eggshell
- → SHOES: Riding boots with
  manure-resistant finish
- → GLOVES: Fitted with nonslip sword grip
- → ROSE (Optional)

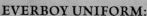

*NOTE: *When the previous School Master began his reign, he created the Blue Forest to prevent any further attacks from the Woods, thus eliminating the need for students to*

Uniforms

NEVERGIRL UNIFORM:

→ SMOCK: Tea-length aged cotton in dead-soul black (by Hunterzombie & Witch, Ltd.)

→ SHOES: Pointy-toe booties with blood-resistant finish

→ ACCESSORIES: Everlasting cobwebs, Festering Wound eau de parfum

NEVERBOY UNIFORM:

→ TUNIC: Authentic cursed sailcloth from the *Jolly Roger*

→ BREECHES: Slender-fit torn canvas in fungus blue

→ SHOES: Torture boots with werewolf-skeleton details

→ KNIFE (Optional; only Dean-sanctioned, professionally blunted weapons allowed and never in the presence of other students)

defend themselves so vigorously. Furthermore, the stiff and unmanageable uniforms of the past were redesigned to facilitate a more practical curriculum.

EVERGIRL UNIFORM:

→ DRESS: Camellia pink taffeta, inspired by the dress Dean Sophie wore to her weekly princess-themed tea parties back when she lived in Gavaldon

→ SHOES: Marble-heeled slippers with rose quartz detail. A flat version is available for Evergirls with dates who are lacking in height.

EVERBOY UNIFORM:

→ VEST: Royal blue velvet (which, in a recent survey that Dean Sophie conducted, was voted the "most dashing" color for princes to wear) with military-style gold epaulets from Smee & Sons' New & Improved Booty Auction

→ BREECHES: 100% Arabian camel hair in alabaster with dragonfly-wing shimmer, because Dean Sophie believes that boys should have a little sparkle too

→ BOOTS: Supple obsidian leather with indestructible palladium buckles, inspired by Dean Sophie's experience masquerading as Filip at the School for Boys

---

*****DEAN SOPHIE'S NOTE:** *Evers and Nevers both voted on whether or not to keep the uniforms from the School Master era or to wear these spectacular new designs created by me, Dean Sophie, in collaboration with Madame Clotilde van Zarachin, the most recent winner of the Gold Award from the Council of Fashion Designers of*

NEVERGIRL UNIFORM:

→ DRESS: Dean Sophie debuted this outfit during a Lunchtime Lecture on "Just Say No to Drab" during her first year as a student and is now proud to see it is the standard of dress for all future Nevers.

→ SHOES: Dean Sophie has had to wade through a lot of muck on her journey to Evil greatness, and she wants all Nevergirls to know that they, too, can trudge through mud in style.

→ ACCESSORIES: This lace veil commemorates the great Lady Lesso, Dean Sophie's predecessor and mentor. The gloves are designed to show off a fresh manicure with one of Dean Sophie's custom nail polishes. (See the Evil Groom Room Menu!)

NEVERBOY UNIFORM:

→ COAT: Sable "Rafal" coat with diamond spikes—an homage to one of the most stylish villains of all time

→ TROUSERS: Real men wear black, unlike the future king of Camelot.

→ SHOES: Each pair of these *jooti*-style loafers is individually crafted by the award-winning cobbler gnomes from the Sand Mountains of Rajashah.

Everwood. Despite vigorous campaigning by Good's Dean in favor of the traditional uniforms, the students of both schools united behind the Sophie–van Zarachin collection, described in detail with my notes on this page. Thank you all for your good taste!

1) **MALE UNIFORM
(EVER & NEVER)**
   School for Boys
   Designed by
   King Tedros of Camelot

2) **FEMALE UNIFORM
(EVER & NEVER)**
   School for Girls
   Designed by
   Dean Evelyn Sader (*deceased*)

---

*NOTE: As we look to the future, we must also take the time to acknowledge the past. The last three years have seen a dramatic evolution, where new leaders questioned the balance between Good and Evil, Boys and Girls, and Old and New.

3) MALE UNIFORM (EVER & NEVER)

School for New Evil

Designed by Master Rafal (*deceased*)
& Dean Aric (*deceased*)

4) FEMALE UNIFORM (EVER & NEVER)

School for New Evil

Designed by Master Rafal (*deceased*)
& Dean Aric (*deceased*)

Now that we have restored peace, we present the archived uniforms of these years—not only as an homage to those who lost their lives defending their school, but also as a reminder of how many battles must be fought on the way to a happy ending.

A NOTE ABOUT TEACHERS

The teaching faculty is the cornerstone of the School for Good and Evil and we are honored to have included them in our discussions about uniform redesign. But unlike the students, the teachers voted down the proposed Sophie–van Zarachin modifications to their own faculty uniforms and preferred instead to retain their centuries-old dress code. In the words of my fellow Dean, I applaud their good taste.

Clarissa Dovey

School for Good

FEMALE

Female teachers of Good are required to wear a high-necked gown in a vibrant color. In order to allow them to express their individual personalities, they are encouraged to add appropriate flair to their uniforms. Suggested accessories include: crystals, beetle wings, baby's breath, freshwater pearls, unicorn braids, or tasteful chain mail.

MALE

Male teachers of Good are required to wear brightly colored suits with slim ties. (Shades of blue are highly discouraged in order to avoid looking like one of the students.) Shoes and belt buckles should be shined regularly, all clothing laundered weekly, and beards kept both neatly trimmed and free of debris.

SCHOOL FOR EVIL

FEMALE

Female teachers of Evil must wear a sharp-shouldered, wing-collared dress. Sinister detailing is encouraged. Hair should be kept in a tight bun or braid, shoe heels sharpened to a deadly point, and nails painted either black or bloodred only.

MALE

Male teachers of Evil must wear one of the dark-colored robes hanging in the Tower of Vice haunted wardrobe. These robes are five hundred years old, never washed, and their stench well earned. (Many a teacher has smothered a student with these robes as punishment.) Faculty are encouraged to accessorize with spikes, chains, and collars, provided they are true testaments to Evil rather than fleeting fashion trends.

School Rules & Discipline

General School Rules
Evers & Nevers

✛ STUDENTS MUST REMAIN IN THEIR ASSIGNED
   SCHOOLS AT ALL TIMES.
> "Good with Good, Evil with Evil" is the golden rule—
> except for joint functions in the Theater of Tales,
> supervised by faculty.

✛ STUDENTS WILL NOT KILL THEIR FELLOW
   STUDENTS.
> Killing stains one's soul permanently. One should only kill
> to save oneself from certain death or to slay one's Nemesis,
> two situations that will NEVER happen within the walls of
> this school (no matter what you may have heard).

✛ STUDENTS ARE FORBIDDEN TO GO INTO THE
   ENDLESS WOODS AFTER DARK.
> Violators will be sent to the Doom Room and/or lose all
> Groom Room Privileges—if you come back alive, that is.

✛ STUDENTS (AS WELL AS TEACHERS *AND* DEANS)
   ARE FORBIDDEN FROM INTERFERING WITH THE
   STORIAN.
> This means: no touching, stealing, manipulating, bribing,
> coughing upon, twisting, shouting at, shaking, tickling,
> smooching, imprisoning, spinning, dueling with, using as
> liquid eyeliner, confiding in, or cursing the sacred pen.

✠ BE AWARE THAT GARGOYLES ARE *NOT* DECORATIONS; THEY HAVE ORDERS TO KILL.

Also, please don't dress them up like fairy princesses while they're sleeping. They don't like it.

✠ READERS AND DESCENDANTS ARE EQUALLY VALUABLE TO THE SCHOOL COMMUNITY.

While you might be born of royal fairy-tale blood, your Reader classmates are just as worthy of an education here as you are. Indeed, they could be the stars of their very own fairy tales one day, no matter how bumbling and ridiculous they may seem at first.

✠ STUDENTS ARE UNABLE TO CAST SPELLS ON SCHOOL GROUNDS UNTIL THEIR FINGERGLOWS HAVE BEEN UNLOCKED.

Any attempt to cast spells with a locked finger will activate a Spellfinder Hex, which will temporarily mogrify you into a Tumbo tree.

✠ STUDENTS WITH THREE CONSECUTIVE LAST-PLACE RANKS IN CLASS CHALLENGES WILL BE **FAILED.**

In a change of rules, all failed students will be sent to dig graves in the Garden of Good and Evil for a semester.

✠ STUDENTS SHOULD NOT ATTEMPT TO MANIPULATE OR CONCEAL THE SWAN CRESTS ON THEIR UNIFORMS . . .

. . . or the swans may be permanently tattooed into your skin (and not necessarily on a part of your body that you'd prefer).

✠ STUDENTS ARE EXPECTED TO BE IN THEIR ROOMS FOR CURFEW AT 10:15 P.M. SHARP.

✛ STUDENTS ARE FORBIDDEN FROM ATTEMPTING TO CROSS THE BARRIER ON HALFWAY BRIDGE.

> Despite Agatha's success in outwitting the barrier several times in previous years, the enchanted wave that monitors the bridge has been restored to Halfway Bay and will quickly lash any trespassers back to their schools.

✛ ONCE STUDENTS HAVE BEEN TRACKED INTO LEADERS, HENCHMEN, AND MOGRIFS (ANIMALS AND PLANTS), THESE DECISIONS ARE **FINAL**.

> Don't want to be a dancing sweet potato? Then you are advised to do your homework and behave in class.

✛ HUNTING OF ANIMALS IN THE BLUE FOREST IS STRICTLY FORBIDDEN.

> Some of them might very well be mogrified alumni.

✛ A PRINCESS AND A WITCH *CAN* BE FRIENDS, BUT STUDENTS SHOULD ENDEAVOR TO FORM ALLIANCES WITHIN THEIR OWN SCHOOLS.

> If you must make friends with someone in the opposing castle, take special care lest he or she turn out to be your Nemesis.

✛ ALL EXTRACURRICULAR CLUBS MUST BE PREAPPROVED BY **BOTH** DEANS.

> This is in response to the recent attempt to create an Evil Secession Society, dedicated to claiming both castles for Evil's domain and relegating Good's campus to a distant outhouse.

✛ ✛ ✛

REPEATED VIOLATION OF THESE RULES WILL RESULT IN IMMEDIATE EXPULSION FROM THE SCHOOL FOR GOOD AND EVIL.

Rules for Evers

Dear New Evers,

Those of you with family members who are alumni of the School for Good might notice that this list of rules and norms is shorter than it was in years past. During her tenure in these towers, Agatha of Woods Beyond challenged many of the more antiquated standards of how Good students were supposed to behave. Her legacy has opened our eyes as to what Good truly means, and our illustrious school is all the better for it.

Sincerely,

Clarissa Dovey

Dean Dovey

* **EVERS MAY NOT TURN PRINCESS UMA'S ANIMAL FRIENDS BACK INTO PEOPLE.**

    Even though Princess Agatha of Camelot is famous for doing this, it upsets the balance of the Woods and requires a greater percentage of new students to be tracked as sidekicks and Mogrifs. In addition, those animals that have been Mogrifs for a long while have likely forgotten how to even be human and prefer to keep their animal forms.

* **EVERS ARE FORBIDDEN FROM CONSUMING CANDIED WALLS AND FURNITURE IN HANSEL'S HAVEN.**

    Temptation is the path to Evil, as *Hansel and Gretel* proves well. In addition, the wanton consumption of candy inevitably leads to rotted teeth, poor discipline, and a general lack of respect both for one's school and one's self.

✸ LOVE SPELLS ARE NEVER ALLOWED, EVEN AFTER FINGERGLOWS ARE UNLOCKED.

> While it is no longer required for Evergirls to attend the Snow Ball with only Everboys and vice versa, the affection between all couples must be genuine and not manufactured.

✸ BE RESPECTFUL OF THE FAIRY GUARDS THAT PATROL THE SCHOOL.

> These are real fairies, unlike the enchanted students of past classes, and they have less patience than their human counterparts. Remember: they bite.

✸ EVERS MUST WEAR THEIR UNIFORMS, UNLESS SPECIFIED OTHERWISE.

> NOTE #1: Girls may not shorten the length of their skirts without official permission from the School Seamstress.
>
> NOTE #2: Boys using the Groom Room pools may not parade around the castle shirtless on their way back to their rooms. There are towels in the Groom Room for a reason.

✸ EVERS MUST RESPECT NATURE.

> This means no campfires, no picking flowers off trees, no littering, no carving names into stones, no collecting birds' nests, no playing "capture the squirrel," no kissing frogs (unless it is part of a sanctioned class exercise), and no maypoles made from vines.

✸ EVERS MUST ALWAYS REACH OUT WHEN ANOTHER STUDENT IS IN NEED . . .

> . . . and not just to those princes and princesses from whom you are hoping to get a Ball invitation.

GROOM ROOM

> **Dean's Note:** We are proud to announce that the Groom Room has been rebuilt after its unfortunate incineration during Dean Sader's reign. In response to those events, the new Groom Room facilities have been made coeducational and gender-neutral in order to facilitate greater interaction and understanding between the sexes. As a result, Everboys and Evergirls may share all amenities (provided the boys do not use this privilege to turn the Groom Room into a sweaty pigsty). Despite these changes, however, the criteria for using the Groom Room remain the same: it is only available to Evers ranked in the top half of their class on any given day.

FITNESS

- Norse Hammer Gymnasium
- Mud-Wrestling Pit
- Salt Water Lap Pool
- Stationary Gondolas for rowing practice (**NEW!**)
- Twelve Dancing Princesses Rhumba Classes (**NEW!**)
- Yuba's Morning Yoga (**NEW!**)

SPA

- Midas Gold Sweat Lodge
- Peasant-themed Tanning Room
- Turkish Baths
- Little Match Girl (or Boy!) Sauna

- The Little Mermaid Lagoon (with waterfall shower)
- Tinkerbell's Fairy Dust Exfoliating Facial (NEW!)
- Golden Goose Skin-Brightening Facial (NEW!)
- Jack's Beanstalk Full-Body Wrap (NEW!)
- Maid Marian's Signature Sherwood Forest Aromatic Body Therapy (NEW!)

HAIR AND MAKEUP

- Red Rose Makeup Stations
- Cinderella's Pedicure Corner
- Rapunzel's Salon (NEW!)
  - Stocked with Goldilocks® Hair Dye
- The Three Little Pigs Blow-Dry Parlor (NEW!)

WARDROBE CONSULTATION AND FORMALWEAR RENTAL

- The Clever Little Tailor's Couture Shop (NEW!)
- The Little Red Riding Hood Costume Collection (NEW!)
- Glass Slipper Shoe Rental (NEW!)
  - All the above are fully equipped with three-way looking glasses.

Rules *for* Nevers

Dearest and Beloved Never Disciples,
Our list of rules is different this year at Evil, too. As your Dean,
I believe you should be treated as intelligent, grounded young
adults rather than as the reckless, bestial hooligans of Evil past.
Our new rules, then, focus on enhancing our collective school
spirit and individual self-esteem.

Nevers Forever!

Dean Sophie

Dean Sophie

- **NO GRAFFITI ON THE SCHOOL FOR EVIL *UNLESS* IT IS IN EXPLICIT SUPPORT OF DEAN SOPHIE'S NEW REGIME AND ARTFULLY RENDERED IN AN AREA WHERE EVERS MAY SEE IT.**

    In which case, it isn't graffiti at all but, rather, a public service.

- **NO POLLUTING THE MOAT.**

    Nobody wants to see your dirty underpants while on a romantic stroll along Evil's shore.

- **NO BULLYING OR THUGGERY OF FELLOW STUDENTS.**

    Bullying is a sign of deep insecurity and weakness of character. That said, if an Ever dares to insult or denigrate you in any way, then consider this rule irrelevant.

- **NO ANIMAL SACRIFICES IN CASTLE STAIRWELLS.**
  I noticed this rule in Lady Lesso's past rule books and
  assume it is there for a reason.

- **NO WHINING TO YOUR MOMMY AND DADDY
  WHEN WRITING LETTERS HOME.**
  They will not be there to help you in the Woods when
  you embark on your fairy-tale journeys. Learn to be
  independent and self-reliant, like a true Never!

- **REGULAR BATHING IS MANDATORY FOR NEVERS.**
  That means actually taking off your clothing and getting
  into the bath. Hiding in the bathroom with the water
  running does not count. SOAP AND WATER MUST
  MAKE CONTACT WITH YOUR BODY.

- **IF YOU ARE REJECTED BY A POTENTIAL
  NO-BALL DATE, THIS DOES NOT MEAN YOU
  CAN KILL THEM.**
  Dean Sophie can speak from experience; violence is
  not the way to show someone you love them. However,
  if your crush has done something truly heinous (e.g.,
  picked your best friend instead of you while both of you
  were disguised as hobgoblins in a "Good or Evil" class
  challenge), a suitable revenge is encouraged, as long as it
  is plotted out of your classmates' sight. A true Never can
  wreak exquisite revenge without bloodshed. Be original.

- **NEVERS ARE FORBIDDEN FROM POSSESSING
  PARTICULARLY PUTRID ITEMS.**
  This includes rotten eggs, fartbombs, skunk glands,
  moldy cheese, bottled foot sweat, and any other materials

that may cause grievous injury to the senses. Why let your odor telegraph that you are evil before you have a chance to work your wiles? No wonder Evil lost for so many years! Listen well: Evil does not equal foul and filthy anymore.

NEVERS ARE FORBIDDEN FROM DISTURBING THE DEAN OF EVIL DURING HER "PERSONAL TIME."

The Dean's office is open for student drop-ins every day from 4:00–4:30 p.m. All other hours are reserved for the Dean's briefings, fittings, meetings, planning, and personal yoga lessons and spa treatments.

NEVERS ARE FORBIDDEN FROM WEARING BLACK-SWAN GOLD AT SCHOOL.

All black-swan gold—otherwise known as "Never gold," magically enchanted to turn your soul to the darkest Evil—must be turned in to the Dean, who will store it for safekeeping.

NEVERS ARE ONLY PERMITTED TO REDECORATE THEIR DORM ROOMS WITH AN APPROVED THEME.

Sample approved themes might include: "Midnight Wonderland," "Forbidden Romance," "Paradise of Evil," or "Glamorous Witches."

GIFTS TO TEACHERS ARE PROHIBITED.

The Dean does not count as a teacher.

EVIL DOOM ROOM

TORTURE MENU

DEAN'S NOTE: *The Man-Wolf who mysteriously disappeared three years ago has been replaced by his much more vicious (and, unfortunately, higher-salaried) cousin. If a Neverboy or Nevergirl is found to be in violation of one of the official school rules, he or she will be sentenced to a torture session in the Doom Room. The Man-Wolf will be selecting from the following list of punishments depending on the severity of the student's offense. Though you might find yourself intimidated, remember that physical hardships can build your character and your strength beyond anything a pampered, prissy Ever can imagine.*

PHYSICAL TORTURE

- Standing on one leg
- Wearing burning-hot shoes
- Dangling upside down
- Smelling the Man-Wolf's feet (NEW!)
- Having arm hairs plucked out one by one (NEW!)
- Getting doused in skunk juice and being shoved into a coffin with a fellow punished student (NEW!)

INSTRUMENTS OF TORTURE

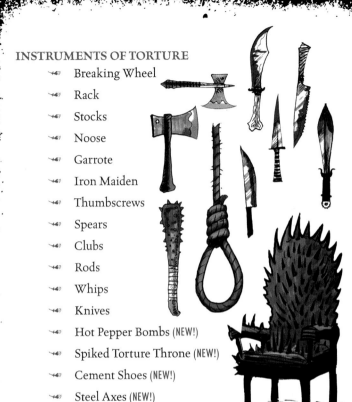

- Breaking Wheel
- Rack
- Stocks
- Noose
- Garrote
- Iron Maiden
- Thumbscrews
- Spears
- Clubs
- Rods
- Whips
- Knives
- Hot Pepper Bombs (NEW!)
- Spiked Torture Throne (NEW!)
- Cement Shoes (NEW!)
- Steel Axes (NEW!)

SHAME AND EMBARRASSMENT

- Having an irremovable "F" emblazoned on your uniform for a week
- A public spanking by Castor during lunch in the Clearing in front of both schools (NEW!)
- Cleaning out the stymph troughs in the Blue Forest for two weeks (NEW!)
- Forced wearing of an Ever's uniform for a full day of Evil classes (NEW!)

THE SCHOOL FOR EVIL
GROOM ROOM

*DEAN'S NOTE: Due to Dean Sophie's campaign for equal beautification, Nevers will, for the first time, have their very own Groom Room, offering top-notch spa services and fitness equipment. All Nevers, no matter what their ranking, will have access to the Groom Room, because Dean Sophie does not want to have to look at a student body that is 50% unkempt.

FITNESS

- Turret Climbing
- Slenderizing Yoga
- Hills in Heels (For Nevergirls Only)
- Demon Kali Dance Hour (For Nevergirls Only)
- Weight lifting in full-body armor (For Neverboys Only)
- Treeboxing in Pine Glen (For Neverboys Only)

SPA

- Cauldron Saunas
- Dragon's Milk Baths
- The Captain Hook Lagoon (with whirlpool)
- Sea-Salt Massage
- The "Dean Sophie Morning Special": grapefruit-seed exfoliation, cacao-and-trout-scale mask
- The "Dean Sophie Evening Special": fish-egg scrub, pumpkin-puree massage, goat's-milk rinse, melon-and-turtle-egg-yolk mask, cucumber elixir

- The Frost Queen's Skin-Paling Room
- The Wicked Witch of the West Skin-Greening Room

HAIR AND MAKEUP

- "Flesh-over" potion for concealing unsightly scabs and scars
- "Flesh-removal" potion for creating new scabs and scars
- Baba Yaga Pedicure Corner
  - Stocked with Dean Sophie's brand-new line of nail colors, including: Reaper Black, Lizard Green, Honora Ochre, Rafal Red, Cucumber Mint, Beetroot, Midnight Sparkle, First-Kiss Blush, Oily Agatha, Dead-Fairy Gray, Dot's Chocolate Brown
- Mother Gothel's Salon
  - Stocked with Bluebeard® Hair Dye
- Cinderella's Stepmother's Vanity Makeup Stations (*For Nevergirls Only*)
- The Sinister Facial Hair Styling Counter (*For Neverboys . . . and some girls*)

WARDROBE CONSULTATION AND FORMALWEAR RENTAL

- Personalized Dean Sophie Makeover
- Rumpelstiltskin's Dancing Shoes Rental
- The White Witch Bone Jewelry Collection

You're gonna love the way you look

HOW TO SURVIVE THE
DÖÖM

MAN-WOLF

Sleek bat-like ears

Mean, ill-tempered, smarter than you

Hairy chest, rippling muscles

Paddle-sized ogre feet

Maintains a steady job

s. WEREWOLF

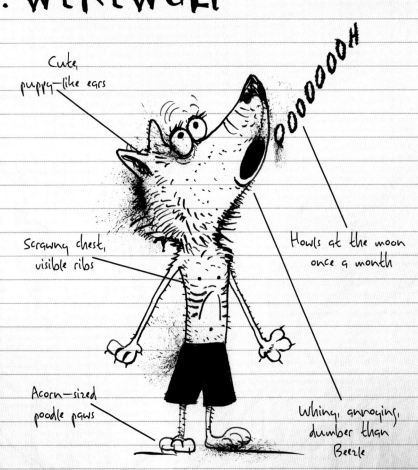

Cute, puppy-like ears

POOOOOOOH

Howls at the moon once a month

Scrawny chest, visible ribs

Acorn-sized poodle paws

Whiny, annoying, dumber than Beezle

IF A TEACHER SENDS YOU TO THE
DOOM ROOM

1. Whatever you do, don't cry, you ninny. Showing your teachers that you're scared of torture will only make them want to torture you more. Instead, you should act like being sent to the Doom Room is a huge relief because it means that you won't have to sit through another minute of their boring classes. In fact, a convincing display of joy might make your teacher reconsider sending you to the dungeon in the first place. If you fail, proceed to #2.

2. When you arrive at the dungeon, regardless of which teacher sent you to the Doom Room, tell the Man—Wolf that it was Castor. Man-wolves <u>hate</u> dogs and will go easy on you or spare punishment entirely. You might even make a new friend.

3. Try to time your Doom Room punishment for between 12:30 and 1:00 p.m. or 7:30 and 8:00 p.m. This is when the Man-Wolf eats his meals, and he takes dining very seriously. If you're particularly talkative and annoying, he'll probably dismiss you unpunished so he can eat in peace.

4. Keep at least one stalk of asparagus on you at all times (but make sure your pet rats don't eat it!). Man-wolves are horribly allergic to the smell and will send you away in a hurry.

5. If you are incapable of successfully deploying any of these four perfectly easy strategies, then TAKE YOUR PUNISHMENT LIKE THE USELESS, INCOMPETENT PEON YOU ARE.

Student Contract

I, _____, a student at the
School for Good and Evil, pledge to remain honest and true to myself
and to my school for the next four years. I will abide by the rules of
Good and Evil, as I understand that these guidelines have set the stage
for every fairy tale in history.

1) The Evil attack. The Good defend.
2) The Evil punish. The Good forgive.
3) The Evil hurt. The Good help.
4) The Evil take. The Good give.
5) The Evil hate. The Good love.

I promise to behave in a manner that brings pride to my fairy-tale
predecessors, but also not to repeat their mistakes. This means that I
will not start any wars, assemble my own army, lie about my identity
to infiltrate the school, try to assassinate the School Master (once
one is appointed), or hide the Storian, even if I only have the best of
intentions. I realize that my instructors are not always perfect, but
they are seasoned professionals, and they only want me to become the
best hero or villain I can be.

I also give my word that I will take responsibility for my actions,
respect my fellow students, and uphold the honor of the School for
Good and Evil, even when I am not within its grounds.

Signed, _____

First-Year Traditions

Dear Ever or Never,

As a first-year student, you will experience our three greatest traditions here at the School for Good and Evil:

- ※ The Trial by Tale
- ※ The Circus of Talents
- ※ The Snow Ball

For the past two hundred years, each of these events had been dominated entirely by the side of Good— until three years ago, when I, a fledgling Never, managed to help Evil win the Trial, the Circus, and its place at the Ball all in the very same year.*

As a result, Dean Dovey and I have attempted to make these traditions more *inclusive*. In the following

---

pages, we will offer you an in-depth look at the rules and history of each event, along with various strategies for success.

Good luck to you all!

Sincerely,

Dean Sophie

Dean Sophie

Note from Professor Dovey: You, the Reader, can decide which side truly won these events. See *The Tale of Sophie and Agatha* for full context.

**Note from Dean Sophie*: You, the Reader, must be aware that no one likes a sore loser. So now it is up to you, dear Nevers, to bring glory to Evil, just like I once did. At last, Evil will have its fair chance at victory!

Trial by Tale

Trial by Tale

OFFICIAL RULES

1.   The top ten Evers and top ten Nevers are required to compete in the Trial by Tale. The competitors will be determined by the school rankings no more than two weeks before the Trial is to begin.

    1a.   Starting this year, each Dean will be permitted to enter one <u>Wild Card</u> into the competition: namely, a student who did not make the ranking cutoff for the Trial but who the Dean still believes will make a worthy combatant.

2.   Entrances into the Trial will be staggered. At sundown, the Ever and Never with the lowest pre-Trial rankings will enter the Blue Forest. Every fifteen minutes, the next-lowest pair will enter until the highest-ranked Ever and Never enter the competition last.

3.   Inside the Forest, Nevers can attack Evers with their special talents and any spell learned in class. Evers can defend themselves with approved weapons and counterspells. Both sides will be subject to obstacles laid throughout the arena by the faculty.

4.   Each challenger will be given an enchanted handkerchief of surrender. It is the challenger's duty to recognize mortal danger and drop his or her enchanted handkerchief when the time comes. The moment this handkerchief touches the ground, the student will be safely removed from the Trial.

5.   Upon the first glint of sunrise, the Deans will call an end to the Trial and the student(s) who returns through the gate alive will be named the winner(s).

6.   The winner will receive five extra first-place ranks in the race for Class Captain. In the case of multiple winners, each student will receive two extra first-place ranks.

> 6a.   NOTE FROM DEAN SOPHIE:
> If the winner or winners are from Evil, they will also receive:
>   1) an autographed copy of *The Tale of Sophie and Agatha,*
>   2) a portrait taken with me to send home to their parents, and
>   3) a private field trip with me to anywhere in the Woods.

> 6b.   NOTE FROM DEAN DOVEY:
> If the winner or winners are from Good, they will also receive the satisfaction of depriving the School for Evil winner of vainglorious bribery. That is surely reward enough.

Blue Forest

Tulip Garden

Pumpkin Patch

Sleeping Willows

Blueberry Fields

Fern Field

Trial by Tale

WINNERS HALL OF FAME

PETER OF NEVERLAND

TOUGHEST MOMENT: "Falling down a killer-rabbit hole"

TIP TO WIN: "There's always a couple of yellow-bellies hiding in the Blue Brook."

SOPHIE OF WOODS BEYOND

TOUGHEST MOMENT: "Being chased by ten Nevers using unapproved spells!"

TIP TO WIN: "Mogrify your way to success."

GUINEVERE OF CAMELOT

TOUGHEST MOMENT: "Watching Lancelot drop his own flag when he and I were the last two left. He sacrificed himself so I could win."

TIP TO WIN: "Winning isn't the goal. Safety is."

HANSEL OF GINNYMILL

TOUGHEST MOMENT: "Throwing my sister Gretel's flag to the ground before a water-dragon scorched her"

TIP TO WIN: "If you're a boy, team up with a girl. They're usually smarter than you."

Circus of Talents

Circus of Talents

OFFICIAL RULES

1.   The Circus of Talents will take place in the Theater of Tales at 8:00 p.m. on the night before the Ball. Attendance is mandatory for students of both schools.

2.   The theater doors will be locked for the entire Circus competition. No teachers will be allowed inside, and no students will be allowed out. Students are encouraged to use the toilet before the program begins.

3.   The two halves of the Theater of Tales will be fully enchanted by the Deans with decorations that inspire school pride for both sides. Students are encouraged to create banners, posters, and other material supporting their respective schools.

4.   Under no circumstances may the audience from either school cross the silver aisle separating the two sides of the theater. Violators will be hung by their toes from the chandelier for the duration of the Circus.

5.   Though the School Master post remains vacant, the Theater of Tales retains the previous Master's enchantments and will magically judge the Circus duels.

6.   The teams for the Circus of Talents will consist of the top ten–ranked students from the School for Good and the School for Evil. These two teams will be selected according to school rankings no more than one week before the competition.

7.   The Circus will consist of ten duels between an Ever and a Never, each performing his or her talent. Talent duels will proceed in order of ranks. They will begin with the tenth pair—the tenth-ranked Ever against the tenth-ranked Never—followed by the ninth-ranked pair, all the way up to the first-ranked pair.

8.   For each duel, the Ever will perform his or her talent, followed by the Never. The theater will select the best talent, anointing a winner and publicly punishing the loser. At the end of all ten duels, the Circus Crown will magically lower onto the head of the student with the most impressive talent overall.

9.   The school of the student who wins the Circus Crown will win the right to host the Theater of Tales in its castle the following year.

WINNERS HALL OF FAME

GRETEL OF GINNYMILL

WINNING TALENT: "Lighting a flame under my feet for five minutes and not sweating a drop"

WORST TALENT ON DISPLAY: "One of the Nevers was in the process of turning his fingers into wooden stakes and accidentally fell off the stage, landed on his hand and impaled his bottom. He couldn't sit down for a week."

JACK OF WOODS BEYOND

WINNING TALENT: "Running and jumping across the top of all the theater benches while managing to touch every single person's head in school, all in under a minute"

WORST TALENT ON DISPLAY: "Some Neverboy killed a pigeon with a noxious fart."

BRIAR ROSE OF MAIDENVALE

WINNING TALENT: "Singing a melody so beautiful that it even made the Nevers cry"

WORST TALENT ON DISPLAY: "This Nevergirl named Rasika tried to blow fire but ended up swallowing it and burping smoke for six months."

SOPHIE OF WOODS BEYOND

WINNING TALENT: "Shattering the theater with a scream, killing wolves and fairies, and destroying half the Good castle, to name a few"

WORST TALENT ON DISPLAY: "I'd say it was a tie between Beatrix's vomit-inducing song to Tedros and Hort writhing on the stage after failing to turn into a wolf and losing all his clothes."

THE EVER–NEVER EXPRESS

THE OFFICIAL STUDENT NEWSPAPER OF THE SCHOOL FOR GOOD AND EVIL

SNOW BALL OR NO BALL? DEANS CHANGE RULES ON WINTER DANCE.

By Kiko of Neverland

IN A STUNNING CHANGE to rules that had been in place for centuries, Dean Clarissa Dovey of Good and Dean Sophie of Evil have agreed that the annual Snow Ball, once strictly the provenance of Good, will no longer belong solely to the Evers. Instead, the right to hold the annual Ball will be awarded to the winning school of the Trial by Tale.

Dean Sophie was the one who put forth the proposal, asking students to vote on the idea in a school-wide referendum. After a week-long campaign, which included a pep rally, ice cream social, and swimsuit fashion show, the measure passed by a single vote—a vote many Evers say was fraudulently changed by Evil's Dean.

"No self-respecting Ever would allow their school to compete for a Ball that's rightfully ours," said Beatrix, a former classmate of Sophie's before Sophie ascended to the rank of Dean. "Besides, doesn't anyone remember what happened the *last* time Evil held a Ball?"

Dean Sophie responded to rumors of vote-tampering with a statement released by her office: "After a hard-fought battle, justice has prevailed. Our focus now is entirely on winning this year's Trial by Tale. Evil looks forward to opening its doors and welcoming Good on the night of the Ball with as much enthusiasm as Good has always welcomed Evil."

When reached for comment, Professor Dovey rolled her eyes.

"This school is not a democracy," she snapped. "Dean Sophie's referendum is complete nonsense. That said, after the events of the last Ball, when the Nevers clearly wanted a dance of their own, it seemed only fair to afford them the opportunity to earn one. But given Good has won the last forty Trials in a row, I think the possibility of Evil ever hosting Good at a Ball is rather . . . *remote*."

Dean Sophie offered a concise retort to her rival Dean: "Let the best woman win."

We, the students, are certainly keen to see what happens.

And maybe a little scared.

The Snow Ball

The No Ball

Greatest Ball Scandals of All Time

Two verses into "The Glory of Love," the song that traditionally ends the Snow Ball, a first-year Everboy named Lancelot cut in and asked Arthur's date, Guinevere, to dance. Guinevere later would say she didn't think twice about accepting the offer. "Lance and Arthur were best friends. Arthur didn't mind at all," she'd tell anyone who asked. But this moment came to foreshadow all that was to come between a King, his Knight, and his Queen.

WHEN JONAH OF HAMELIN CHARMED A SPITTING
cobra with his pipe at the Circus of Talents, earning him
the title "The Pied Piper of Hamelin," every student in
school assumed he'd be the first Never to win the Circus
Crown. But when the Crown lowered onto a less-talented
Evergirl's head instead, Jonah publicly fumed, vowing
revenge at the Snow Ball the following night. And indeed,
just as the dance began, Jonah used his pipe to summon
every rat from the Endless Woods, desecrating Good's
Grand Hall and ending the Snow Ball before it even
started.

THE 25ᵀᴴ ANNIVERSARY OF THE SNOW BALL SHOULD
have been special, with Good's Grand Hall transformed
from a traditional ballroom into a wintry ice rink. Evers
trained for months in Etiquette and Grooming classes
to waltz on ice with their dates. Unfortunately, the
lake water imported into Good Hall for the dance also
contained a substantial school of Wish Fish. Trapped
without warning, they rebelled by gathering under the
ice and revealing the Evers' most illicit wishes. With
everyone's true feelings about each other revealed, the
Ball quickly degenerated into chaos.

IN THE MOST SCANDALOUS MOMENT OF ALL, TEDROS OF
Camelot fell for Sophie's Evil trap on the night of the
Snow Ball and, in front of the entire school, nearly
killed his own princess with an arrow to the heart. If
it wasn't for Sophie's timely intervention, Tedros may
have never found his happy ending.

The Evers Snow Ball

GIRLS HALL OF FAME

ANYA OF WOODS BEYOND
(AKA THE LITTLE MERMAID)

SOPHIE SAYS: "Anya's look was a showstopper at her Snow Ball and continues to inspire other lively young ladies throughout the Endless Woods. We love the bright colors and the jewelry that was handmade by some of Anya's underwater friends!"

AGATHA OF WOODS BEYOND
(AKA AGATHA OF CAMELOT)

SOPHIE SAYS: "Due to an unfortunate series of misunderstandings between Good and Evil, Agatha never got to attend her Snow Ball, but even still, she looked quite the Ever at the Circus of Talents the night before. The fairies in the Groom Room allegedly collapsed from exhaustion after pulling off 'the most revolutionary make-over in school history,' but their efforts were well worth it because Agatha's elegant ensemble took everyone's breath away. It should be noted, however, that Agatha's lifelong best friend tried for *years* to make her over but she never *listened*, and it's not fair to give all the credit to the fairies, because many elements of Agatha's outfit are *strangely* reminiscent of *original* looks that your very own Dean Sophie has worn in the past."

BOYS HALL OF FAME

BOGGLE AND BOBEE
OF PUMPKIN POINT
(AKA TWEEDLEDEE AND TWEEDLEDUM)

SOPHIE SAYS: "Twins are rare at SGE, and we can safely say that these two created double the spectacle at the Snow Ball. There was nothing 'dum' or ho-hum about the flamboyant colors and patterns—very risky but very chic."

KAVEEN OF SHAZABAH
(AKA PRINCE OF SHAZABAH)

SOPHIE SAYS: "While he may have angered several professors by arriving on a recalcitrant elephant, Kaveen still managed to have a *major* style moment at his Snow Ball. His tunic was made by the Stubborn Silkworms of Pifflepaff Hills; his slippers were pure hammered white-gold from the rich mines of Putsi."

School History

Normally, the Ever Never Handbook includes a detailed school history section, excerpted from Professor August Sader's *A Student's History of the Woods*. But you'll be reading plenty of that book in your classes, and let's be honest: Is there anything more boring than an official history? Besides, Professor Sader is dead (he never liked me much anyway, so excuse me if I say this with dry eyes), which means it's time for fresh blood in our history department. Blood that's young and virile and *exciting*.

Unfortunately, with the deaths of Professor Sader as well as Dean Evelyn Sader and Master Rafal—the history position seems a bit cursed, doesn't it?—we've found it difficult to fill the post for our new class. Indeed, no matter what salary or additional perks we offer, Professor Dovey and I have found the door slammed in our faces by every viable candidate. It was only in the eleventh hour that I saved the day (as usual) by calling upon a reliable friend who accepted my offer to teach history to you, the Evers and Nevers of the new class. Despite Professor Dovey's rather vocal protests to the contrary, I think that your new history teacher is *completely*

---

qualified for the position. After all, he has the three most important criteria necessary for such a post: 1) he knows the school intimately; 2) he came running the moment I called, even at the risk of such a cursed job; and 3) he's proved himself 100% compliant with my input and direction.

So with the utmost confidence, I turn this section over to this freshly minted Professor of History, a man of exceptional lineage and dignity . . . Professor Hort of Bloodbrook, who will now offer you his fully comprehensive and not-at-all-boring history of the School for Good and Evil.

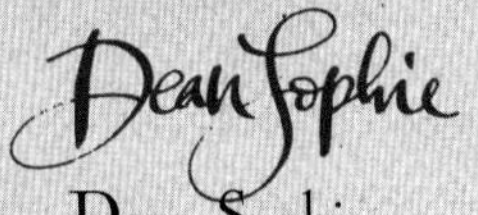

Dean Sophie

Dean Sophie

A HISTORY OF THE STORIAN

By Professor Hort of Bloodbrook

LONG, LONG AGO, BEFORE THERE WAS MAN, THERE WAS THE PEN. . . .

And so the handsomest boy in the world was born, and his name was Hort.

OH, I AM SO HANDSOME.

THIS PEN, NAMED THE STORIAN, WAS WHERE ALL FAIRY TALES CAME FROM. . . .

IN FACT, SOME PEOPLE THOUGHT THE PEN MADE MAN UP TO BEGIN WITH.

???

AM I MAN OR STORY?

SOON THERE WERE TWO CAMPS: PEOPLE WHO THOUGHT MAN CREATED PEN. AND PEOPLE WHO THOUGHT PEN CREATED MAN.

MAN!

PEN!

ALL THIS OVER A WRITING UTENSIL!

RAAAAAAAAAAH!

RAAAAAAAAAAAH!

THE FIGHTS GOT BIGGER, WITH BOTH SIDES WANTING THE STORIAN FOR THEMSELVES.

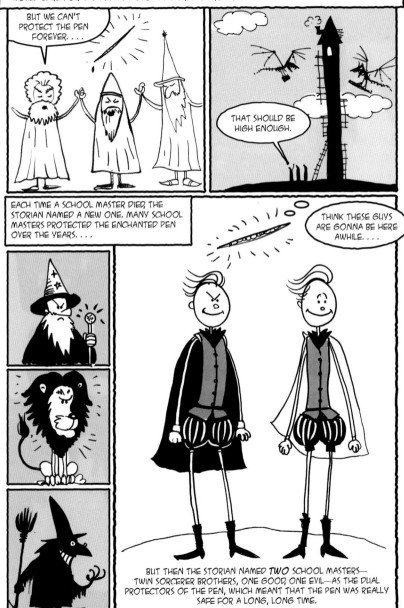

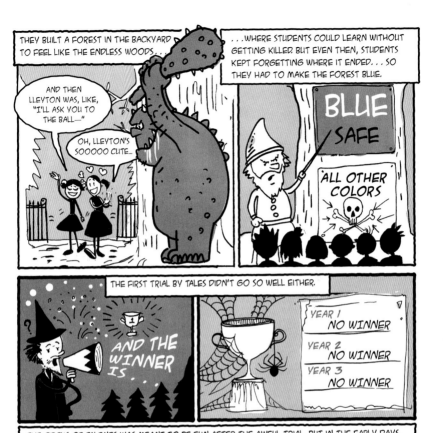

THEY BUILT A FOREST IN THE BACKYARD TO FEEL LIKE THE ENDLESS WOODS...

...WHERE STUDENTS COULD LEARN WITHOUT GETTING KILLED. BUT EVEN THEN, STUDENTS KEPT FORGETTING WHERE IT ENDED... SO THEY HAD TO MAKE THE FOREST BLUE.

AND THEN LLEYTON WAS, LIKE, "I'LL ASK YOU TO THE BALL—"

OH, LLEYTON'S SOOOOO CUTE...

BLUE
SAFE

ALL OTHER COLORS

THE FIRST TRIAL BY TALES DIDN'T GO SO WELL EITHER.

AND THE WINNER IS...

YEAR 1
NO WINNER

YEAR 2
NO WINNER

YEAR 3
NO WINNER

THE CIRCUS OF TALENTS WAS MEANT TO BE FUN AFTER THE AWFUL TRIAL, BUT IN THE EARLY DAYS, NEVERS WEREN'T TRAINED IN SPECIAL TALENTS AND USED SKETCHY SPELLS TO ENTERTAIN THEIR CLASSMATES INSTEAD...

FOR MY TALENT, I WILL TURN INTO A BAT.

BOOM

THIS LED THEM TO START A SPECIAL TALENTS CLASS IN THE SCHOOL FOR EVIL.

WHY DO YOU GET A TALENTS CLASS AND WE DON'T?

BECAUSE YOU SUCK!

A HISTORY OF ROMANCE

By Professor *Hort of Bloodbrook*

SINCE I AM NOT MUCH OLDER THAN YOU, I THOUGHT IT MIGHT BE HELPFUL TO EXPLAIN TO YOU HOW ROMANCE WORKS AT THE SCHOOL FOR GOOD AND EVIL.

HORT'S GUIDE to LOVE

THE BEST WAY IS TO TELL YOU A TRUE STORY, THOUGH I WILL CHANGE THE NAMES OF THOSE INVOLVED IN ORDER TO PROTECT THEIR IDENTITIES.

BORT   LOPHIE

ONCE UPON A TIME, BORT MET LOPHIE WHEN THEY WERE DROPPED INTO THE SCHOOL FOR EVIL. IT WAS LOVE AT FIRST SIGHT.

I WANT TO TOUCH YOUR HAIR!

GET AWAY FROM ME, YOU CREEP!

BORT DID EVERYTHING FOR LOPHIE. HE WAS NICE TO HER. HE HELPED HER WITH HER HOMEWORK. HE EVEN LET HER BUNK WITH HIM WHEN HER ROOMMATES TRIED TO KILL HER.

BORT, HELP MEEEEEE!

BUT NO MATTER WHAT BORT DID, LOPHIE STILL TREATED HIM LIKE MOAT SCUM.

BUT IT'S MY ROOM TOO!

97

LOPHIE EVEN STOLE HIS PAJAMAS.

RIP

IT WASN'T LOPHIE'S FAULT SHE COULDN'T SEE BORT WAS HER REAL TRUE LOVE. SHE HAD BEEN DUPED INTO FALLING FOR KEDROS, A FAILED PRINCE WHO NO ONE LIKED BECAUSE HE WAS DUMB AND PRETENTIOUS.

U + ME = CALCULUS

HOW ROMANTIC!

LOPHIE!

KEDROS!

HAGATHA!

?

THEN KEDROS FELL IN LOVE WITH LOPHIE'S BEST FRIEND, NAMED HAGATHA. BUT EVEN THEN, LOPHIE ONLY HAD EYES FOR KEDROS.

BORT TRIED TO MAKE NEW FRIENDS TO TAKE HIS MIND OFF LOPHIE.

FINALLY, A NEW FRIEND WHO ISN'T LOPHIE!

ACTUALLY, I'M LOPHIE IN A BOY'S BODY.

WHAT DOES KEDROS HAVE THAT I DON'T?

IN THE END, BORT HAD HIS HEART BROKEN AGAIN.

SO BORT DECIDED TO TRY TO BECOME LIKE KEDROS.

I CAN FEEL MY BRAIN CELLS DYING.

LOPHIE WAS DEFINITELY ATTRACTED TO BORT NOW.

GOSH, BORT'S LOOKING GOOD . . .

Illustrious
Alumni

LEADERS

BRIAR ROSE OF MAIDENVALE
Best Subject: Beautification (Top Scores in
 Nighttime Skin Care)
Founder of the SGE Slumber Party Club
Life Motto: "If life hands you spindles,
 weave a sweater."

Briar Rose of Maidenvale

**RITA OF NETTLE FOREST
(AKA RED RIDING HOOD)**
Best Subject: Senior Citizen Care (Focus on denture-
 friendly baking)
President of the SGE Blue Forest Trailblazers
Life Motto: "A wolf in any other clothes still smells
 like a wolf."

Rita of Nettle Forest

JACK OF WOODS BEYOND
Best Subject: Language Arts (Fluency in Giant)
Lead Gardener, SGE Amateur Topiary
    Enthusiasts (Winner, Circus of Talents)
Life Motto: "Every bean has a silver lining."

Jack of Woods Beyond

PINOCCHIO OF HAMELIN
Best Subject: Creative Writing
Chairperson, SGE Association for the Liberation
    of Marionettes (SALOM)
Life Motto: "I live life with no strings attached."

Pinocchio of Hamelin

CATHERINE OF FOXWOOD
Best Subject: Uglification (Specialty: Wart Growth)
First Place, SGE Lethal-Dish Cooking Contest,
    Category: Vegetarian
Life Motto: "Don't put all your poisoned apples in one
    basket."

Catherine of Foxwood

RUMPELSTILTSKIN OF BLOODBROOK
Best Subject: Curses and Death Traps (Thesis Paper
    on "Impossible Riddles" published in the
    Netherwood Villain Digest)
Life Motto: "If you stamp your feet and cry as well,
    you will find yourself IN HELL."

Rumpelstiltskin of Bloodbrook

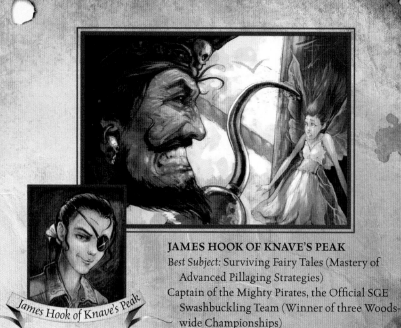

JAMES HOOK OF KNAVE'S PEAK

Best Subject: Surviving Fairy Tales (Mastery of
Advanced Pillaging Strategies)

Captain of the Mighty Pirates, the Official SGE
Swashbuckling Team (Winner of three Woods-
wide Championships)

Life Motto: "The hook is mightier than the sword."

James Hook of Knave's Peak

**GERTRUDE OF RAVENBOW
(AKA HANSEL AND GRETEL'S WITCH)**

Best Subject: Evil Hideout Construction
(Final Project: Building with Edibles)

Record Holder, Annual SGE Hot-Crog-
Eating Contest

Life Motto: "If it can't scream, don't eat it."

Gertrude of Ravenbow

HELPERS

MERLIN OF GINNYMILL
Best Subject: Independent Study
in Gnome Biology
Trusty Skill: On-the-road
nourishment

**TOPAZ OF WALLEYE
SPRING** (AKA **Tinkerbell**)
Best Subject: Fairy-Tale
Chemistry (Magical-Dust
Infusion)
Trusty Skill: Pot and kitchen
utensil repair

SMEE OF NEVERLAND

Best Subject: Herbal Healing
  (Concentration: Seasickness
  Prevention)
Trusty Skill: Ship-based servitude

BROOT OF ROCH BRIAR

Best Subject: Archery while
  mounted on a stymph
  (learned in preparation for
  the Second Great War)
Trusty Skill: Laying hidden
  trip wire

MOGRIFS

OSIRIS OF RUNYON MILLS (AKA "Baby Bear" from *Goldilocks and the Three Bears*)

Secret Talent: Can hold sparklers between his toes

KIANNA OF PUMPKIN POINT (AKA Aladdin's "Magic Carpet")

Secret Talent: Effectively disguising herself as an end table

YVONNE OF KINGDOM KYRGIOS (AKA "Pea" from *The Princess and the Pea*)

Secret Talent: Hiding in human ears, nostrils, mouths, armpits, belly buttons, and other orifices

CHESTER OF PUTSI (AKA "the Cheshire Cat" from *Alice in Wonderland*)

Secret Talent: Chasing shiny things and/or balls of yarn

Obituaries

Good

LETITIA OF MAIDENVALE (AKA SNOW WHITE)—Brutally slain by the zombie Wicked Queen in the Cottage White Massacre. Snow will be remembered for her genuine kindness, her fierce loyalty, and her award-winning limericks.

ALBRECHT OF ALBION WAY (AKA SNOW WHITE'S DWARF #1)—An unfortunate victim of the devastating Cottage White Massacre. His surviving friends and family describe him as driven and very good at sweeping.

BERNHARD OF BORA CORIC (AKA SNOW WHITE'S DWARF #2)—Another casualty of the Cottage White Massacre. He leaves behind a vast collection of feathers.

CONRAD OF CARVASSO CANYON (AKA SNOW WHITE'S DWARF #3)—Died in the Cottage White Massacre along with Snow White and his six longtime roommates. Conrad liked to whistle.

DIETRICH OF DILLAVORE (AKA SNOW WHITE'S DWARF #4)—One of the eight people who died in the senseless Cottage White Massacre. Villagers fondly remember his handmade holiday decorations and his excellent mulled wine.

EMMERICH OF ETERNAL SPRINGS (AKA SNOW WHITE'S DWARF #5)—He had just completed a seven-month correspondence course in Ancient Troll Dialects when the Wicked Queen struck him dead in the Cottage White Massacre.

Franz of Frostplains (aka Snow White's Dwarf #6)—A victim of the Cottage White Massacre, Franz died doing what he loved: carving a wooden bust of his beloved pet turkey.

Gottfried of Gillikin (aka Snow White's Dwarf #7)—He perished heroically in the Cottage White Massacre while trying to protect his roommates. Sadly, Gottfried will never be able to complete his goal of swimming across every creek in the Woods.

Rapunzel of Roch Briar—After overcoming cruel imprisonment and going into hiding at a young age, Rapunzel finally found happiness with her beloved Prince Townsend. Her life was cut tragically short when Mother Gothel returned from the dead and flung both Rapunzel and Townsend from the tower in which they had made their family home. She is survived by her two small children.

Townsend of the Boglands (aka Rapunzel's prince)—Driven by pure love, Townsend overcame seemingly insurmountable obstacles to be with Rapunzel. He lived a happy life with his beloved, and they died clasped in each other's arms.

Ella of Maidenvale (aka Cinderella)—The late Ella remains one of the bravest, and yet the most misunderstood, fairy-tale characters of all time. Her Evil Stepmother tore her and her dear stepsisters apart; Ella was never able to repair the resulting wounds. Later in her life, she was instrumental in helping Sophie and Agatha reconcile, which restored peace to the Woods and cemented Ella's place as a feminist icon in fairy-tale history.

Keir of Netherwood (aka Tom Thumb)—As a young man, Tom never let his diminutive stature get in the way of his pursuit of adventure. Tom had retired from royal service when his Nemesis plucked him right out of his home and ate him. Sadly, Tom was not able to escape the giant's digestive system this time.

CORDELIA OF JAUNT JOLIE (AKA THE MILLER'S DAUGHTER)—The Miller's Daughter eventually became the queen of Kingdom Percival after marrying the king, who demanded she spin straw into gold. Queen Cordelia went on to become a famed alchemist, thus bringing great riches to her kingdom. Unfortunately, zombie Rumpelstiltskin's surprise attack led to her untimely demise.

WILLIAM OF BREMEN (AKA BILLY GOAT GRUFF #1)—The eldest Billy Goat Gruff is best known for his successful outwitting of the horned troll who tried to prevent him from crossing a bridge. He was grazing with his son and grandson when the aforementioned troll caught them by surprise and consumed them all. He leaves behind a wife and five grand-"kids."

WILLIAM OF BREMEN JR. (AKA BILLY GOAT GRUFF #2)—The successor to his father's name and legacy, the second Billy Goat Gruff used to make villagers laugh with his spot-on imitation of the horned troll that he, his father, and his grandfather outsmarted. Unfortunately, the troll had the last word.

WILLIAM OF BREMEN III (AKA BILLY GOAT GRUFF #3)—The youngest of the three Billy Goats Gruff had just graduated a few years before his death. He loved playing stickball with the village children and made it a point not to eat their storybooks. He will be missed.

CATTRICK OF CARABAS (AKA PUSS IN BOOTS)—After graduating, Puss ascended to great heights as a royal feline and later, a fashion designer and Woods-wide trendsetter. Though Puss believed that he had heard the last of his Nemesis, the ogre, the beast returned from the dead and swallowed Puss—and his famous boots—whole.

Anya of Woods Beyond (aka the Little Mermaid)—Anya hailed from the modest village of Gavaldon, after which her fairy tale became one of the most beloved throughout the Woods and under the sea. Young girls saw her as a trailblazer for her courageous decision to leave home in search of true love. Anya had recently started a foundation for the education of young Mer-People, and it will continue in her memory.

Professor August Sader—The youngest member of the line of Sader Seers, who made a tremendous sacrifice in order to restore balance to the Woods. He is the originator of the Reader Prophecy, the most famous prediction to emerge from his family. Professor Sader is also famous for writing A *Student's History of the Woods*, which is still a seminal text for every student. Sader tragically perished after the School Master attacked him during *The Tale of Sophie and Agatha*.

Thannis of Ooty (aka the Library Tortoise)—He served as the librarian for the Library of Virtue for nearly 700 years, 699 of which he was sleeping, snoozing, napping, and/or eating lunch. He did take a particular liking to Agatha and was instrumental in helping her defeat Dean Evelyn Sader. However, the tortoise paid dearly for his courage when Dean Sader unceremoniously threw him out the window.

Tristan of Avalon Towers (Student)—Tristan was a warm, caring young man who loved to dance and appreciated all things beautiful. These days, it is rare for a student to die during his time at the School for Good and Evil, but the last class's journey was not exactly in line with tradition. Former Dean Aric of the School for Evil killed Tristan (while he was disguised as his alter ego, Yara) during the Trial by Tale between the School for Girls and the School for Boys.

Nicholas of Ginnymill (Student)—Tan and handsome, Nicholas came to school from a long line of Evers, as his parents and his three older brothers were all graduates of the School for Good. He fought valiantly against the School Master in the Second Great War but sadly was struck down in the prime of his life.

EVIL

LADY LEONORA LESSO—After graduating from the School for Evil, Lady Lesso served as the Dean of this same school for over twenty years. Though her school suffered loss after loss, Lady Lesso remained devoted to maintaining the balance between Good and Evil. The School for Good and Evil was the only place where Lady Lesso was truly happy; her friendship with Clarissa Dovey was the one constant that she could depend on. During the Second Great War, she risked her life to vanquish the School Master and bring peace to the Endless Woods. She died at the hands of her own son while defending the castles, even though her best friend was by her side until the very end. Our school is a stronger, more united place because of Lady Lesso's sacrifices, and we won't soon forget her.

DEAN EVELYN SADER—Though she was related to the line of Sader Seers, Evelyn herself did not present any extraordinary abilities. She made up for this with her magical butterflies, through whom she spied on others across the Endless Woods. She began her academic career when her half brother, August, secured her a position as a history teacher at the School for Evil. However, in a wayward attempt to prove her loyalty to the School Master, Professor Sader incited a civil war between Evers and Nevers, which led to her eviction. She returned to the School for Good and Evil ten years later as the Dean of the School for Evil after proving herself useful to the School Master. Once she had fulfilled her purpose, however, the School Master executed her. She will be remembered for her excellent style and her nasty habit of interfering.

ARIC OF BLOODBROOK—Even before his mother abandoned him in a cave in order to become the Dean of the School for Evil, Aric had no internal sense of decency and/or balance. Driven by anger and hate, he found great satisfaction in torturing, beating, and terrifying students. He died at the hands of Clarissa Dovey as she valiantly tried to save her best friend, Lady Leonora Lesso, from the blade of Lady Lesso's own son. We can't think of anyone who is going to miss him.

CALLIS OF NETHERWOOD—The Storian chose a lovely young witch named Callis for *The Tale of Callis and Vanessa* shortly after she started teaching Uglification at the School for Evil. The fairy tale sparked the School Master's interest, and he pursued her; but Callis, dreaming of true love, escaped from the school and found herself in the nonmagical village of Gavaldon. It was there that she found what she was looking for . . . but in an unexpected place. As the adoptive mother of Agatha of Woods Beyond, Callis finally felt real, enduring love. She died heroically while saving Agatha and her prince, Tedros of Camelot, from the village Elders. She is survived by Agatha of Camelot, Tedros of Camelot, and Reaper. The villagers of Gavaldon will forever be indebted to Callis for her healing potions and salves, as well as for her noble sacrifice that saved them all from obliteration (even though they couldn't see it at the time).

GRIMM OF PASHA DUNES—At the School for Evil, Grimm was tracked as a Henchman. However, instead of entering his own fairy tale, he was hired to apprentice with new Evil students during the first-year Sidekick Challenge. This turned out to be a rather large error of judgment on the part of the administration, as Grimm was a free thinker and did not enjoy following orders. He died as he lived: a wild hellion wreaking havoc.

BEEZLE OF DIRT ROAD—A former student of the School for Evil who was tracked as a Henchman and was eventually hired as a maintenance dwarf at his alma mater. He died after being head-butted into the bay by a zombie ogre, and Castor already led a short memorial, so there's not much more to say here (and we're running out of space).

RAFAL (OBITUARY INCLUDED AT THE INSISTENCE OF DEAN SOPHIE, COMPOSED BY DEAN SOPHIE)—Although Rafal killed his brother and started a long conflict in which many of my friends, teachers, and classmates were destroyed, I cannot deny his importance in our school's history . . . or in my own fairy tale. Rafal was a man who knew what he wanted. He had an impeccable sense of style and understood the importance of luxury in living a satisfying life. He certainly had some strange and dangerous ideas about how to govern the School for Good and Evil, but I will always remember him for making me a queen—and for starting a war over me. The things we do for love!

HOW NOT TO DIE
By Castor & Pollux

The last year has been the deadliest in our school's history, despite the administration's best efforts to keep students safe from harm. In addition to the new security measures (detailed throughout this *Handbook*), we know that our dearly departed alumni would want you to learn something from their deaths. To honor them, we've compiled this handy list of tips on how to survive your time here at school, Evers and Nevers alike.

Pollux Says: Do inform a teacher if you see an armed stranger lurking about the halls (zombie villains included). It's possible that the stranger is just someone's parent or a guest speaker for Evil, but it's also possible that he or she is here to kidnap you.

Castor Says: DON'T PLAY POLKA MUSIC TOO LOUD BECAUSE I HATE POLKA MUSIC AND I MIGHT KILL YOU.

Pollux Says: Do lock your door at night to avoid all potential threats.

Castor Says: DON'T GET NEAR OPEN WINDOWS WHILE FIGHTING WITH FRIENDS. THE MOST COMMON CAUSE OF DEATH AT SCHOOL IS WHEN KIDS LOSE THEIR TEMPER AND THROW THEIR FRIENDS OUT WINDOWS.

Pollux Says: Do make sure that you are fully prepared for battle and don't underestimate your opponent!

Castor Says: DON'T TAUNT PEOPLE ON THE BATTLEFIELD BY PULLING YOUR PANTS DOWN BECAUSE SOMEONE DID THAT TO ME ONCE AND I ATE HIM.

Pollux Says: Do invest in a decent suit of spiked armor, especially if your Nemesis is substantial in size.

Castor Says: DON'T FIGHT A DRAGON WITHOUT GETTING YOUR ARMOR FIRE-PROOFED FIRST. DUH.

FOR MOGRIFS—*Pollux Says:*
Do urge your animal friends to wear bells while they graze in case you get separated in the meadow.

FOR MOGRIFS—**Castor Says:** DON'T KEEP BELLS ON IF YOU'RE BEING CHASED BY A MURDERER. THEY WILL TINKLE WHEN YOU'RE TRYING TO HIDE AND YOU WILL DIE.

THE SCHOOL FOR GOOD AND EVIL

BY THE NUMBERS

Since the founding of our school more than five hundred years ago, our students have seen a great deal of triumph and have also overcome obstacles that ranged from mildly discomfiting to life threatening. You, as a new student, are inheriting an impressive legacy that encompasses the best—and worst—traditions that fairy tales have to offer.

The School for Good

Statistics supplied by DEAN CLARISSA DOVEY

In the past five hundred years, **99%** of the Snowbell Peace Prize winners have been graduates of the School for Good . . .

. . . and **98%** of Woods-wide Beauty Pageant winners (in the Human, Animal, and Plant categories) have been graduates of the School for Good (it would be 100%, but the White Witch was quite fetching in her day).

82% of School for Good graduates from the Leader track have gone on to replace a tyrannical ruler, thus bringing joy and socioeconomic equality to their respective kingdoms.

91% of School for Good graduates have made selfless sacrifices that spared the lives of others.

In addition, former Evers have . . .

- rescued over 10,000 damsels in distress . . .
- befriended nearly 20,000 animals . . .
- sung 100,000 sweet, lilting melodies . . .
- woven 50,000 fresh daisy chains . . .
- danced at 40,000 balls . . .
- won 25,000 sword fights . . .
- defeated 10,000 evil curses and spells . . .
- smothered 800 rapidly spreading fires . . .
- and saved 4,500 villages from pillaging.

THE SCHOOL FOR EVIL

Statistics supplied by DEAN SOPHIE

Over the past five hundred years, 98% of School for Evil graduates could have used a makeover (see Dean Dovey's note about the White Witch). Indeed, if they had received proper training in personal grooming, the results would be quite different. Luckily, the new regime at the School for Evil has already taken steps to address this. Case in point: the usage of the School for Evil bathing facilities has already increased by 56% this term.

87% of all Wanted posters issued throughout the Endless Woods have depicted School for Evil graduates. The other 13% were probably issued in error, because, let's face it, today's princes and princesses pose a threat to absolutely *no one*.

100% of individuals sentenced to the dungeons for Crimes Against Humanity (Enchanted *and* Unenchanted) have been graduates of the School for Evil. Please note that this is the only 100% achievement in the history of the School for Good and Evil.

73%

of current School for Evil students dream of *ruling* kingdoms and not just terrorizing them. Dean Sophie's new curriculum will certainly convert the remaining 27% by the time they graduate.

In addition, former Nevers have . . .

put over 10,000 damsels in distress . . .

eaten nearly 20,000 cute animals . . .

silenced over 100,000 cloying princesses' songs . . .

incinerated 50,000 fresh daisy chains . . .

sabotaged 15,000 balls and other celebratory events . . .

won the *other* 25,000 sword fights . . .

cast 10,000 evil curses and spells . . .

started 1,000 rapidly spreading fires . . .

and pillaged over 6,000 villages (You can't save them all, Evers!)

HOW TO PRANK

1. Send invitations to a secret Evers' Ball to be held in the Clearing at midnight. Fill the clearing with fire ants.

2. Before the Everboys' swordplay class, dip all the training swords in a bottle of Skunk Stench (there's always at least 3 fresh vials of it in Professor Manley's cupboard). The resulting duels will be most entertaining!

3. Infiltrate the Laundry after curfew and deface the Evers' uniforms with Evil graffiti (like giant skulls, bleeding demons, or anything else that makes Evergirls cry.) The Evers will have to decide between skipping class until they get clean uniforms or embracing their new look. Either way Evil wins.

AN EVER

4. On the day of the Snow Ball, put a note in the most popular Evergirl's room, telling her she's won a special haircut from Cinderella's hairdresser. When she arrives at the Groom Room, you'll disguise yourself as this hairdresser and proceed to shave the Evergirl's head.

5. During the annual Sidekick Challenge, when each Ever and Never is given a creature to take care of for a week, find the most popular Everboy's sidekick and bribe it to give the Everboy a public beating during lunch in front of both schools. The boy's social status will never recover, and you will be thoroughly entertained.

6. The Evers always go first during the Circus of Talents, so right before the show begins, smear the entire stage with snake oil. Word of advice: don't sit in the first row.

HISTORICAL ARTIFACTS
Gallery of Good

ANIMAL FLUENCY EXAM
(Letitia of Maidenvale,
aka Snow White)

**HOLDEN OF RAINBOW
GALE** (aka Jack's Beanstalk)

**WHALE-TOOTH
NECKLACE** belonging to
Pinocchio of Hamelin

A **CLUMP** belonging to
Agatha of Woods Beyond

PERSONAL DIARY
(Valeria of Pasha Dunes,
aka the Little Match Girl)

**BANNER CELEBRATING
ANNABEL OF WOODS
BEYOND** (aka Beauty) after
she won the Circus of Talents
with a death-defying demon-
stration of lion taming

FIRST-YEAR BATHROBE
(Rita of Nettle Forest,
aka Red Riding Hood)

**HEINRICH OF
NETHERWOOD** (aka
Cinderella's Pumpkin Carriage)

The EXHIBITION

Enchanted mirror belonging to Leandra of Frostplains (aka the Frost Queen)

Conklejohn of Necro Ridge (aka the Scorpion from The Scorpion and the Frog)

Contescu of Pifflepaff Hills, Parikhar of Tombstone Bridge, Vlad of Cobblepond (aka the three Henchmen of the Wicked Queen of Foxwood)

Essay on "Morality of Murder" by Griselda of Ravenbow (aka the Wicked Witch of the West)

# of EVIL HISTORICAL ARTIFACTS

Slippers belonging to
Angus of Woods Beyond
(aka Jack's Giant)

First-year arrival outfit
belonging to Sophie of
Woods Beyond

Vera of Woods Beyond
(aka the vine of thorns that
blinded Rapunzel's Prince)

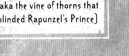

Handmade pure gold trunk
(Rumpelstiltskin of Bloodbrook)
[Warning: Do not try to lift!]

EVER AFTER

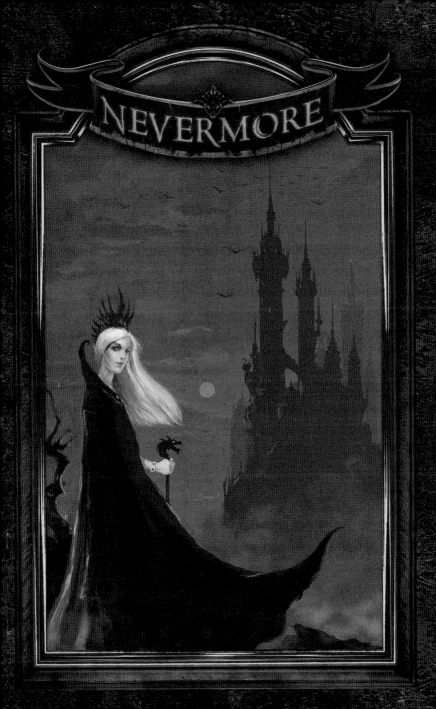

Time Capsule

STUDENT MOGRIFIES INTO WOODS' FIRST-EVER GOLDEN-EGG-LAYING GOOSE

WHILE NATASHA OF Maidenvale was a student in the School for Good, she was tracked as a Mogrif. After graduating last year, she was supposed to be one goose amongst twenty in a fairy tale entitled *The Un-lucky Farmer*. However, the titular farmer turned out not to be so unlucky after all. Two days ago, the goose formerly known as Natasha laid a solid gold egg. News of this incident, which can only be called a miracle . . .

continued on page B6

Drogan of Murmuring Mountains receiving an unwanted makeover from some mischievous fairies

Evergirls filling the Groom Room, anxious to get pedicures in preparation for their Snow Ball

PROFESSOR EVELYN SADER EVICTED AFTER ALLEGATIONS OF "CRIMES AGAINST STUDENTS"

PROFESSOR EVELYN SADER, who was hired to teach history at the School for Evil this year, has been forcefully removed from her position after a war broke out between Evers and Nevers. Luckily, no major injuries were sustained on either side, but the school administration agreed that the upheaval was completely unnecessary and that Sader deserved to . . .

continued on page A10

Peter of Neverland showing why he is permanently banned from the Flowerground

SCHOOL TO START ACCEPTING READERS—WILL THEY SURVIVE?
"NOT IF I CAN HELP IT," SAYS DEAN OF EVIL.

WITH THE APPOINTMENT of the new School Master, students and teachers have already experienced a number of modifications to the school's culture. The biggest change, however, is that the school will now be accepting Readers from unenchanted kingdoms. The only person who has been vocally opposed to . . .

continued on page C3

INGERTROLL INFESTATION UNDER SCHOOL'S BRIDGES—COUPLES BEWARE!

IT IS SPRING, AND LOVE IS IN the air at the School for Good and Evil. However, a number of young Evergirls and Nevergirls have been mysteriously flung off bridges while strolling with their beaux. Pest Control has discovered that a rogue group of Ingertrolls, normally found in Netherwood and Runyon Mills, have somehow . . .

Volkan of Nottingham taking his Evil Hall Monitor duties very seriously

Student Life

Weekly Meal Plan
THE SCHOOL FOR GOOD

DAY	SUNDAY	MONDAY	TUESDAY
Breakfast	• Buttermilk porridge • Jam tarts • Honeycomb bars	• Gingerbread pancakes • Wild strawberries • Licorice-clove tea	• Olive oil and sardine toast • Maple-sugar crepes • Raspberry curd
Lunch	• Hazelnut hot cross buns • Hard-boiled eggs • Rosewater plums	• Smoked-trout sandwiches • Rampion salads • Strawberry soufflé	• Rutabaga bisque • Parsley slaw • Lavender petits fours
Dinner	• Steak pie • Cinnamon-carrot salad • Dandelion fizz	• Rabbit sausages • Dusted biscuits • Aniseed éclairs • Pomegranate juice	• Ham hock pie • Asparagus with truffle sauce • Peppermint meringues
Dean Dovey says	*"Porridge, buns, eggs, and pie keep you healthy by and by!"*	*"If you feel fatigued and low, perk up with a bit of clove!"*	*"Maple and sugar make a sweet treat, but be sure to eat plenty of meat!"*

HESTER SAYS

No wonder Evers walk around looking like they sucked on lemons. Give me a pail of gruel any day.

WEDNESDAY	THURSDAY	FRIDAY	SATURDAY
• Baked eggs with cheese • Oatcakes with quince jam • Vanilla milk	• Sliced peaches • Mint whipped cream • Boysenberry–goat cheese croissants	• Lemon-ginger tarts • Dried figs • Rhubarb turnovers	• Currant cakes with honey butter • Sweet-cream fritters • Hot cocoa
• Broiled herring • Haricots verts • Sugarplums • Cherry tea	• Lamb sandwiches • Saffron couscous • Almond mousse	• Assorted miniature meat pies • Baked aubergine • Mint lemonade	• Watercress quiche • Radish-fennel stew • Blackberry doughnuts
• Dressed salmon • Sweet potato mash • Gold-leaf macaroons	• Squab cassoulet • Orange-beet salad • Cranberry jellies	• Goose curry • Lentil salad • Pistachio sorbet • Violet water	• Apricot lamb chops • Foie gras with rosemary crisps • Citron cream puffs
"Eat salmon and herring, both gifts of the sea, and wash it down with some sparkling tea!"	*"Nothing is more pleasing than peaches and cream, and our orange-beet salad tastes like a dream!"*	*"For most of your ailments, there is a cure—eating well will help you for sure!"*	*"For the past one hundred years, Evers have greeted this menu with cheers!"*

Weekly Meal Plan
THE SCHOOL FOR EVIL

NOTE FROM DEAN SOPHIE:

Upon reviewing my predecessor's menus and experiencing one too many buckets of gruel myself, I overhauled the entire menu to protect our dear Nevers' palates. After painstaking experimentation and discussions with the top chefs throughout the Woods, I present to you the new and improved School for Evil health plan!

STRICTLY FORBIDDEN

| Milk | Gruel | Potatoes |
| Cheese | Salt | Shellfish |

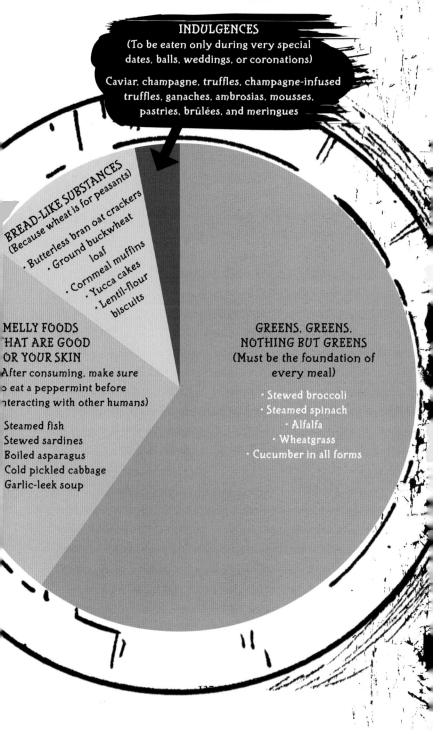

INDULGENCES
(To be eaten only during very special
dates, balls, weddings, or coronations)

Caviar, champagne, truffles, champagne-infused
truffles, ganaches, ambrosias, mousses,
pastries, brûlées, and meringues

BREAD-LIKE SUBSTANCES
(Because wheat is for peasants)

· Butterless bran oat crackers
· Ground buckwheat loaf
· Cornmeal muffins
· Yucca cakes
· Lentil-flour biscuits

**SMELLY FOODS
THAT ARE GOOD
FOR YOUR SKIN**
(After consuming, make sure
to eat a peppermint before
interacting with other humans)

Steamed fish
Stewed sardines
Boiled asparagus
Cold pickled cabbage
Garlic-leek soup

**GREENS, GREENS,
NOTHING BUT GREENS**
(Must be the foundation of
every meal)

· Stewed broccoli
· Steamed spinach
· Alfalfa
· Wheatgrass
· Cucumber in all forms

Note from Hester: My dear Nevers: With all the helpful advice I have given you thus far, it might seem unfathomable that I have any gifts left. And yet, here is where I save not only your sanity, but also your lives. Because the one thing you'll need to survive school more than anything else is this. . . .

TAKE-OUT MENUS!

Since the new Dean has banished everything edible from the Evil Supper Hall, I suggest ordering from these fine establishments on the sly. You can usually bribe the wolves with a greasy side dish to let the Delivery Gnome into the castle.

The DUNGEON Deli

Breakfast:

2 mini-Stymph eggs any style (digested, contaminated, or stepped on)   4.50p

    with snakecon and hoof fries   6.50p

    with corned teeth   7.75p

Omelet (Possible mix-ins: scorpion tails, razorwood, troll bunions, mosquito wings, earwax, the cold sweat of prisoners, seasonal Mogrif droppings)

    (with 2 mix-ins)   8p

    (with 3 mix-ins)   9p

Handcakes or stench toast with fearup and gutterbutter   9p

Sandwiches

The "Aric": Skullami, glazed bunny-glands, toe-volone cheese, and poi ivy between two slabs of granite

The "Beezle": Pepperpony, meatdolls hairinara sauce on a sliced log

The "Mona": Prickly vines, cobra sp and aspara-pus in a green garte wrap

The "Anadil": A grilled-sneeze san with snakecon and pleghmato

The "Hort": Roast bees, grandma hemlock paste, and cobra wa

THE PIZZERIA of PUNISHMENT

APPETIZERS:
Garlic Head (6 mouse heads per order)   6p
Squashed Chinchilla Salad   6p

ENTREES:
Spaghetti and Mucusballs   10p
Carcass Calzone   10p
Lizard-agna   10.50p
Scabioli with Blood Sauce   12p

SPECIALTY PIZZAS:
The Bluebeard: 12p
Thin-crust pie with blue cheese, gravel, fish guts,
baby tears, and sliced skullami

The White Witch:
Regular-crust pie with tripe, pustules, dried maggots,
fingernail shavings

Vine of Thorns (Vegetarian):
Deep-dish pie with slippery twigs, poisonroot, moss,
gravel mash

Make your own (Choose up to 4 toppings):

Dried maggots
Skullami
Baby tears
Gravel
Wasp stingers
Roach antennae
Nymph talons

Pustules
Slippery twigs
Poisonroot
Fish guts
Ants
Blobs of slime
Jackal whiskers

DUMPY'S DERELICT DUMPLING HOUSE

APPETIZERS:
Sour & Dour Soup   2p
Phlegm Drop Soup   2p
Crusty Barnacle Salad   2.50p
Scallion Pancakes   3p

Dumpy's Famous
Dumplings (2 per order)   6p

Choose your filling:
  Earthworm Stir-Fry
  Minced Crog Tail
  Moo Shu Poo
  Tadpole Gizzards

Can be served moldy or scorched

ENTREES:
Mole-Brain Noodles   8.50p
Leg Foo Young   9p
General Crow's Pigeon   9p
Reeking Duck   10p

The
10 BEST & WORST THINGS TO TURN INTO
CHOCOLATE

BY DOT OF NOTTINGHAM

(Recent Graduate of the School for Evil)

BEST

1) Cornish hen
2) Barrel (preferably one filled with oranges)
3) Grandfather clock
4) Lantern (Remove the oil first!)
5) Brass doorknob

6) Saddle

7) My father's sundial (accidental,
   but delicious—at any time of day!)

8) Executioner's axe (unused)

9) Lute

10) Circus crown (Don't tell Dean Sophie.)

WORST

1) Gunpowder

2) Albemarle the Woodpecker
   (It won't work, and he'll bite you.)

3) Textbook (They're enchanted to taste like
   rat droppings if you try. YUCK.)

4) Rusty nail

5) Iron cauldron belonging to Hester
   (She attacked me with a ladle.)

6) Gravestone (It's not worth being haunted.)

7) Hort's pants (They smell, no matter what.)

8) Executioner's axe (used)

9) Fire of any kind

10) Repeat #9 for emphasis. It's really a *very*
    bad idea.

Academics &
Daily Life

CURRENT FACULTY & ADMINISTRATION
THE SCHOOL FOR GOOD

DEAN CLARISSA DOVEY
Good Deeds

Favorite Hobby: "I am quite the chess player. Lady Lesso and I had an ongoing rivalry, which I led 133 games to 22. I hear Dean Sophie is eager to take Leonora's place in our matches. Does she even know how to play?"

PRINCESS UMA
Animal Communication

Favorite Animal: "I used to have the sweetest little white bunny named Roscoe, who slept in my bed. But then he got bitten by a vampire bat."

RUMI ESPADA
Swordplay & Weapons Training
Best Student: "Lancelot had peerless skill and an innate sense of chivalry. He beat Arthur so badly once in a duel that he purposely lost the rematch in order to repair their friendship."

ALEKSANDER LUKAS
Chivalry & Grooming
Tip on Grooming: "If your breeches are sagging so low that we can see your underpants, your future looks very dim."

YUBA THE GNOME
Surviving Fairy Tales
Food Tip: "If you run out of meerworms while traveling in the Woods, toasted crickets make a suitable (and often tastier) meal."

EMMA ANEMONE
Beautification
Biggest Regret: "Missing the Snow Ball when I was a student because no boy asked me. Ever since then, I've committed myself to empowering the female sex whether or not a girl chooses to have a male companion."

POLLUX
Princess Etiquette
Extracurricular Activity: Founder & Adviser of the Ever-Never Anti-Bullying Alliance (ENABA), dedicated to extinguishing the mistreatment of those with unique characteristics, specifically canines who do not exemplify traditional norms of masculinity.

HORT OF BLOODBROOK
History of Heroes
Advice for Evers: "Make friends with the weirdos. There's usually more of them than the popular kids, which means you'll actually be the popular one."

ALBEMARLE THE WOODPECKER
Groom Room Attendant
Pet Peeve: "Boys and girls who flirt with each other in the hot tubs. Such a *cliché.*"

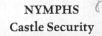

NYMPHS
Castle Security

FAIRIES
Patrol & Discipline

The School for Evil

DEAN SOPHIE OF WOODS BEYOND
Curses & Death Traps
Current Hobby: "I'm working on the musical for next year, entitled *Queen, Icon, Goddess.* I won't tell you who it's about for fear of spoiling it, but let's just say, I know a lot about the person. Tee-hee."

BILIOUS MANLEY
Uglification
On the Importance of Being Ugly: "Despite the new campaign for Evil 'beauty and hygiene,' a true villain knows it's what's on the inside that really matters."

CASTOR
Henchmen Training
Retirement Plans: "Dogs don't live all that long, so I'd like to get a house in the country soon and raise my own sheep and eat 'em for every meal."

SHEEBA SHEEKS
Special Talents
Special Talent: "Training young idiots who spend too much time whining like nincompoops instead of actually making useful contributions to the Evil cause."

HORT OF BLOODBROOK
History of Villainy
Advice for Neverboys: "Girls like boys who act brooding and deep but who also happen to have nice muscles and cool clothes, so yeah, good luck figuring that one out."

WOLVES
Patrol & Discipline

GARGOYLES
Castle Security

THE SCHOOL FOR GOOD AND EVIL

Course Catalog

Year One

EVERS ONLY
(Note: All classes required)

GOOD 101. BEAUTIFICATION (GIRLS ONLY)
PROFESSOR ANEMONE

A comprehensive introduction to female empowerment through beauty, with focus on the texts *Winning Your Prince* and *The Recipe Book for Good Looks*. Sample units include: Developing Your Smile, Ball Fashion, Inner Radiance, and Princess Posture. Those who find the pursuit of beauty a shallow or worthless endeavor will leave with a new, more enlightened perspective. (Poor attitudes, however, will not be tolerated, nor will eating of the classroom's candy walls.) Requirements include: weekly tests, practical challenges, and a year-end makeover project.

GOOD 102. PRINCESS ETIQUETTE (GIRLS ONLY)
POLLUX

Imagine a prince who finds a girl of his dreams . . . only to discover she's a clumsy, spoiled, and incompetent mess! Thankfully, every first-year Evergirl takes my seminal course, which will mold you into a princess of whom even the most unyielding mother-in-law can be proud. (Not all of you will end up princesses or even living in proximity of one, however.) Units will include: Dancing for Dummies, Ladle or Spoon: The Science of Utensils, Voice Modulation, and more. Requirements include: periodic challenges, attendance at seasonal dances, and helping Professor Pollux find a suitable body on which to attach his head.

GOOD 103. SWORDPLAY & WEAPONS TRAINING
(*NOW FOR BOYS AND GIRLS)
PROFESSOR ESPADA

With Evil's reliance on dirty tricks, your greatest defense will be both an iron will and a faultless education in honorable fighting. Together, boys and girls will develop dexterous abilities with: swords, daggers, spears, bows and arrows, maces, cannons, battering rams, and more obscure weapons. All students will use blunted training weapons until they pass the designated Competency Challenge. In addition, any Ever incapable of handling weapons in a mature and responsible manner will be stripped of Groom Room Privileges and sent to the Dean for further punishment.

GOOD 104. ANIMAL COMMUNICATION
(*NOW FOR BOYS AND GIRLS)
PRINCESS UMA

I've never taught boys before, and I couldn't be more excited! Welcome, welcome to the most fun class you'll have at school, where you'll meet all my best friends, including stymphs and squirrels and horses and all the other creatures big and small that live in our Blue Forest. We're even getting a new supply of Wish Fish this year, so you'll be able to participate in our most famous challenge! Other units include: How to Deal with a Rabid Rodent, Mogrif or Animal, and Common Animal Language Phrases (e.g., "Which way is north?"). Those with animal allergies should inform Dean Dovey so you may be inoculated prior to class.

GOOD 105. CHIVALRY & GROOMING (BOYS ONLY)
PROFESSOR LUKAS

As a result of Good's long winning streak, Everboys have become increasingly complacent and arrogant. This strict and demanding class will restore your potential to have a real Ever After that people not only remember, but also value as a model for their own lives. Sample units will include: Proper Footwear for Quests, Manly Scents, Sewing for Boys, Introduction to Female Thinking, and more. Requirements include: weekly challenges, a family genealogy project, and choosing one Evergirl on whom to practice various chivalrous techniques throughout the year.

GOOD 106. PHYSICAL EDUCATION (BOYS ONLY)
ALBEMARLE

Open Period in the Groom Room for boys to work on athletic skills, including: weight lifting, wrestling, wall climbing, hammer throwing, and more. See the Groom Room menu for a list of all available activities.

GOOD 107. HISTORY OF HEROES
PROFESSOR HORT

This newly revamped class won't be boring like most history classes. I haven't really read A Student's History of the Woods and don't know all that much about stuff that happened before I was born, so there won't be any lecturing or anything like that. Instead, I'll be bringing in a bunch of friends as guest speakers, like Hester of Ravenwood, Anadil of Blood-brook, Dot of Nottingham, Agatha of Woods Beyond, Tedros of Camelot, Chaddick of Foxwood, Kiko of Neverland, and more to tell you everything they know about history and school and other useful stuff. There are no requirements for this class, other than you don't throw food at me or say anything negative about me when Dean Sophie is around.

GOOD 108. GOOD DEEDS
DEAN DOVEY

Good Deeds are about more than good looks, good clothes, and good behavior. Good Deeds are about actually contributing something to the Woods in which we live. Sample units will include: Respecting Your Elders, Underprivileged Mogrifs, and Replanting the Woods. Though this class is after lunch, those caught sleeping through class or mumbling groggily when called upon to answer a question will be swiftly punished with toilet-cleaning duties.

NEVERS ONLY
(Note: All classes required)

====

EVIL 101. UGLIFICATION
PROFESSOR MANLEY

For most of your life, you've been judged by how you look. This is true of both Evers *and* Nevers. But while Evers cultivate these looks and thereby weaken their souls, here at the School for Evil, I teach Nevers how to free themselves from the burden of their mundane shells. For an hour a day, I will make you as ugly as possible, anointing you with shingles, warts, and pox; making your hair fall out; or even turning your entire face upside down. Uglification is a great weapon of Evil, allowing you to shape-shift and elude Good's defenses. But to use this weapon wisely, you must allow yourself to *feel* ugly and not be scared of those feelings, particularly when others react to the way you look. This is the villain's true path to empowerment . . . and to freedom. Indeed, by uglifying each and every day, you will realize how fragile and impermanent your looks truly are—and how your personality, values, and inner strength are far more enduring and crucial to your happiness.

====

EVIL 102. HENCHMEN TRAINING
CASTOR

HENCHMEN TRAINING IS A VERY SIMPLE CLASS. I BRING SCARY HENCHMEN, AND YOU TRY NOT TO DIE. SOMETIMES KIDS DIE BECAUSE THEY DON'T PAY ATTENTION TO WHAT I SAY, SO IF YOU DIE, IT'S YOUR FAULT, AND I DON'T WANT TO GET A LETTER FROM YOUR PARENTS AFTERWARD, 'CAUSE I'LL JUST TELL THEM YOU WERE AN EMBARRASSMENT AND THE WORLD'S BETTER OFF WITHOUT ANOTHER BUNGLIN' NEVER.

EVIL 103. CURSES & DEATH TRAPS
DEAN SOPHIE

At first, I was going to reinvent this course so it included fashion make-overs, Evil self-esteem affirmations, and a complete history of my own life, including staged autobiographical monologues every Friday. . . . But then I remembered how I came to be the great villain that I am. And it all began in Lady Lesso's class. Once upon a time, in a frozen room, I discovered my Nemesis: a person who gets stronger as I get weaker, a person who would prevent me from ever finding peace, a person I had to destroy. . . . Now it is your turn to see if you too will find your greatest enemy. But even if you don't find your Nemesis in my class, it is my duty to prepare you for your Evil future, just as Lady Lesso once prepared me. Sample units include: Princess Traps, Poisonous Potions, Prince Emasculation, Manipulative Spells, and more.

EVIL 104. HISTORY OF VILLAINY
PROFESSOR HORT

Um, see Good 107. It'll be like that. But more Evil.

EVIL 105. SPECIAL TALENTS
PROFESSOR SHEEKS

Greetings, young sprouts! Each of you is born with a special Villain Talent, whether you know it or not. And no, a talent is not burping the alphabet, making bathroom noises with your armpit, or eating live gold-fish. A talent is something that emanates from your soul and is unique to *you*. In our last graduating class, we had a variety of talents: a girl with a demon tattoo that attacked people . . . a girl who could turn anything she touched into chocolate . . . a boy who could manifest ten different heads . . . a girl who could make her rats grow forty feet tall. . . . But surely you can do even better! Requirements include: keeping a daily log of Talent Progress, performing in weekly talent duels against other students, and competing in the Circus of Talents if you make Evil's team.

EVERS & NEVERS
(Note: Required Class)

GOOD 109/EVIL 106. SURVIVING FAIRY TALES
VARIOUS FOREST GROUP LEADERS

Students will be divided into 16 Forest Groups, with 5 Evers and 5 Nevers in each group, helmed by a leader from the Endless Woods. The class takes place in the Blue Forest and will pit Evers against Nevers in weekly challenges, as well as train all students in units such as Navigation, Monster Combat, and Plant Identification in order to prepare you for your graduation into the Endless Woods. Trial by Tale training will also happen in your respective Forest Groups.

Year Two

EVERS ONLY
(Note: All classes required)

GOOD 201. ADVANCED BEAUTIFICATION & GROOMING
PROFESSOR ANEMONE

In this intermediate workshop for both boys and girls, Evers will work in teams to develop their own clothing and accessories lines. With periodic input from the professor, you will create a complete collection for your fashion label, including menswear and womenswear. The course will end with a runway competition, which will take place in front of the entire school, featuring you and your team members as models of your new apparel. The winning team will have its line produced by Cinderella's Mice Designs, Ltd.

GOOD 202. GOVERNANCE & KINGDOM TRAINING
PROFESSOR LUKAS

In this coeducational class, Everboys and Evergirls will be taught how to run a kingdom, should they manage to ascend to the rank of prince or princess after graduation. Units of study include: Kingdom Treasuries, Advisory Council Structure, Scandal Management, and more. Assignments are highlighted by a yearlong project on a specific kingdom, which you will visit and study before presenting a series of proposed improvements to its acting leader in front of the kingdom's court. Usually these kingdom leaders are appreciative of our visiting students. A few Evers, however, have come across as arrogant or impertinent . . . and lost their heads as a result.

GOOD 203. HISTORY OF FAIRY TALES
PROFESSOR HORT

I thought I knew all my fairy tales, until I met the League of Thirteen—a group of famous old heroes—during my adventures last year. Which got me thinking . . . if we have so many famous alumni, why not get them to answer your questions about what living through a fairy tale is really like? So for this second-year class, we'll be having heroes and villains come in each week to give you their personal tips on how to best survive your future fairy tales.

GOOD 204. ADVANCED ANIMAL LINGUISTICS
PRINCESS UMA

In the second year, you will choose a specific animal language for fluency. Requirements include: weekly proficiency exams (with your animal partner), plus after-school study of Animal Language Recordings that can be rented from the Everwood Zoological Society in your chosen species for a nominal fee. Most popular languages picked include: Horse, Sheep, Cat, Canine, Rabbit, Frog, Deer, Cow, and Bird (including various sub-tongues).

GOOD 205. GOOD DEEDS: FIELD TRAINING
DEAN DOVEY

An intensive field internship dedicated to community service. All students must prepare and submit a proposal in the spring of their first year, testifying as to the Good Deed on which they plan to focus during their second year. Upon approval, they will spend 10 to 15 hours a week on location, working towards their service goals. Past projects include: Organizing a School for Good and Evil Health Fair, Staging a Marathon to Raise Money for Flowerground Refurbishment, Adopting and Fixing a Pothole in the Endless Woods, Tomb Upkeep in the Garden of Good and Evil, Repairing a Wishing Well, and Serving as a Museum Tour Guide at a Local Everwood-Sponsored Institution.

GOOD 206. EVER CHOIR & ORCHESTRA
POLLUX

In the first year, special attention was placed on the ability to dance and move with a modicum of grace. In the second year, we focus on vocal and instrumental abilities, culminating in a grand performance for the Duke and Duchess of Putsi at their annual Easter Ball. All girls must choose either a vocal or instrumental part to dedicate themselves to over the coming year. (Since boys always choose to play the drums, I will assign their parts myself.)

NEVERS ONLY
(Note: All classes required)

EVIL 201. UGLIFICATION: DISGUISES & DEFORMITY
PROFESSOR MANLEY

After a full year of uglifying, you are now prepared in Year 2 to begin using the principles of Uglification to defeat your Ever enemies. Sample units include: Shape-shifting for Maximum Disgust, Noxious Body Scents, Cronyism (aka Old Woman Disguises to Fool Treacly Princesses), and more.

EVIL 202. HENCHMEN: FIELD TRAINING
CASTOR

IF YOU DIDN'T DIE IN MY LAST CLASS, NOW YOU'LL GO INTO THE ENDLESS WOODS AND MEET WORKING HENCHMEN WHO WILL JUDGE YOUR CHALLENGES AND DECIDE IF YOU'RE WORTH THE DIRT YOU STAND ON. UNLIKE THE FIRST YEAR, IF YOU MAKE A MISTAKE, I WON'T BE THERE TO SAVE YOU LIKE SOME CODDLING AUNTY. MAKE A MISTAKE AND THESE HENCHMEN WILL SQUASH YOU TO SMITHEREENS, JUST LIKE IN REAL LIFE. HENCHMEN JUDGES WILL INCLUDE: GIANTS, OGRES, TROLLS, GENIES, ROGUE DWARVES, AND MORE.

EVIL 203. ADVANCED CURSES & DEATH TRAPS
DEAN SOPHIE

Whether summoning a flock of murderous ravens, weaving magical snakeskin, or unleashing a lethal howl, I've always dispatched Evers with creativity and grace. In this second-year course, I'll be teaching my most private spells for defeating a Nemesis, with units including: Screams from the Soul, Invisibility Capes, Prince Manipulation, and more. Limited to the 10 best students of my choosing.

EVIL 204. HISTORY OF FAIRY TALES
PROFESSOR HORT

(See Good 203, but it'll be more focused on the fairy tales that Evil won. Lady Lesso swore these fairy tales existed, even though no one remembers them and I haven't the faintest clue where to find them. . . . Ummm, but I'll find out before class starts!)

EVIL 205. ADVANCED SPELL CASTING
PROFESSOR SHEEKS

Dear little kiddies, you have gone from sprouts to little bushes. Now I will turn you into trees! Not literally, of course (unless you are absolutely useless, in which case, you will be tracked as a tree in your third year). In the first year, you had your fingerglow unlocked by your Forest Group Leaders before you learned basic weather, water, and Mogrification spells. But in this class, you'll graduate to: Force Spells, Protection Spells, Energy Spells, Time Spells, and Death Spells (theory only). Given the delicacy and danger of our endeavors, the Doom Room's Man-Wolf will sit at the back of our classroom and publicly punish any student who indulges in mischief or tomfoolery.

EVERS & NEVERS

GOOD 207/EVIL 206. SURVIVING FAIRY TALES
VARIOUS FOREST GROUP LEADERS

Forest Groups will remain the same in the second year as your teams of 5 Evers and 5 Nevers move into the Endless Woods to begin simulating the real-life conditions you will face after graduation. All students must sign an additional waiver that denies Group Leader liability in the case of injury, mutilation, or death.

Year Three

EVERS ONLY

(*Note: Students may enroll in five of the following classes, provided they fulfill the requirements for entry. The last class, "Surviving Fairy Tales," is still required of all Evers and Nevers.)

GOOD 301. BEAUTIFICATION/GROOMING:
EXPRESS FOR SUCCESS
PROFESSOR ANEMONE

Elective seminar that uses miming, classical improvisation, Reiki, chakra crystals, and facial yoga to develop authentic self-expression.

GOOD 302. BEAUTIFICATION/GROOMING:
ADVANCED STRENGTH TRAINING
PROFESSOR LUKAS

Intensive physical training regimen, with visits to the local Ever army military barracks for weekend boot camps. Only students who pass a diagnostic physical will be allowed to enroll.

GOOD 303. BEAUTIFICATION/GROOMING:
RADIANCE RETREAT
PROFESSORS ANEMONE & LUKAS

By invitation only. The top 5 Boys and top 5 Girls in the Ever class will be enrolled in this advanced seminar, which will take them to the greatest temples of Beautification and Grooming in the Endless Woods. Field trips include visits to: the Salt Lagoons of Shazabah, the Golden Spa of Ooty, the Hot Stone Caves of the Murmuring Mountains, and more.

GOOD 304. DANCE WORKSHOP: WALTZ & RONDEL
POLLUX

Note: Partners required for enrollment.

GOOD 305. DANCE WORKSHOP: INTERPRETIVE MOVEMENT
POLLUX

Every future ruler needs to let off some steam after a hard day of ruling a kingdom. This is your opportunity to relax your shoulders, slather yourself in body paint, and shake your bottom to the beat. Students will leave with a better sense of their bodies and souls, and the inner strength to be able to face any challenge (including abusive twin siblings who share your body or a world that does not recognize your many talents).

GOOD 306. ANIMAL COMMUNICATION: STUDY ABROAD
PRINCESS UMA

Students fluent in a particular animal language are invited to travel and live with an animal family in the Endless Woods. See list of available host families in the Dean's office.

GOOD 307. ANIMAL COMMUNICATION: MOGRIF GROOMING & TRAINING
PRINCESS UMA

For students tracked as Mogrifs only—a chance to grow comfortable with your new form.

GOOD 308. GOOD DEEDS: SIDEKICK TRAINING
PROFESSOR DOVEY

For students tracked as Helpers—a seminar dedicated to the role of a proper sidekick and how to balance deference with self-respect.

GOOD 309. GOOD DEEDS: LEAD THE WAY
PROFESSOR DOVEY

For Leaders only—a comprehensive philosophy of governance for those seeking to rule their own kingdoms. Focus will be on governing for the people rather than one's own ego.

GOOD 310. HISTORY SEMINAR: HISTORY OF WAR
PROFESSOR HORT

Professor Dovey said I had to have an advanced seminar option for students wanting to study history as a possible profession (Really? People *do* that?), so I racked my brain for things I like reading and thinking about, and all I could come up with was girls and war, but Professor Dovey said I can't do a whole class about girls because it's sexist, so we settled on "History of War." It'll be cool, though—lots of blood and backstabbing and people's heads on spikes. Maybe we'll even have Sophie as a guest speaker since she fought in the Good-Evil War, Boy-Girl War, and Old-New War . . . but only if you remember to say nice things about me while she's here.

NEVERS ONLY

(*Note: Students may enroll in 5 of the following classes, provided they fulfill the requirements for entry. The last class, "Surviving Fairy Tales," is still required of all Evers and Nevers.)

EVIL 301. UGLIFICATION SEMINAR: MIMICRY
PROFESSOR MANLEY

The ultimate disguise? Taking on the face and body of your Nemesis, so you can impersonate them at will. Learn how in this advanced Uglification class. Open only to those tracked as Leaders, with enrollment capped at 15 to enable close teacher-student attention.

EVIL 305. UGLIFICATION: LEADER "LOOKS"
DEAN SOPHIE

Instead of Professor Manley, I will now be teaching this advanced seminar, dedicated to helping those tracked as Leaders find a suitable "look" for their grand and ambitious futures. Where Professor Manley stressed the importance of uglifying in a *traditional* sense, I believe in a more fluid interpretation of what it means to be a villain. After all, with Evil no longer restricted to the gruesome and grotesque, there is nothing stopping you from being both intimidating *and* alluring . . . like me. The class will culminate in our interrupting Good's Advanced Beautification Runway Show with our own parade of Evil beauties.

EVIL 303. UGLIFICATION SEMINAR: HENCHMEN "LOOKS"
PROFESSOR MANLEY

For those tracked as Henchmen—a seminar that uses Uglification principles to help you develop an odious and frightening appearance that will make your Evil Leader both proud and eager to use you in the front lines of battle.

EVIL 304. INDEPENDENT STUDY:
SIDEKICK CHALLENGE ORGANIZER
CASTOR

EACH YEAR THERE'S A SIDEKICK CHALLENGE WHERE WE HAVE TO PAIR EVERY SINGLE EVER OR NEVER IN SCHOOL WITH A SIDEKICK, WHO THEY HAVE TO KEEP ALIVE FOR A WEEK. THIS IS A LOT OF WORK FOR ME TO DO ALONE. NOT ONLY DO I HAVE TO FIGURE OUT WHICH SIDEKICK GOES WITH WHICH STUDENT, BUT I HAVE TO FIND ALL THE SIDEKICKS AND THEN GO TELL THEIR PARENTS IF THEY DIE BECAUSE OUR STUDENTS ARE TOO STUPID TO KEEP 'EM BREATHING FOR SEVEN DAYS. WHICH MEANS I NEED A FEW DECENT NEVERS TO TAKE OVER THE CHALLENGE SO I CAN HAVE A YEAR OFF FOR ONCE. I ONLY TAKE NEVERS TRACKED ON THE HENCHMEN TRACK, AND IF I CHOOSE YOU, YOU DON'T HAVE TO PARTICIPATE IN THE BLASTED CHALLENGE (YOU'RE WEL-COME). ONCE THE CHALLENGE IS OVER, YOU CAN SPEND THE REST OF THE YEAR SLEEPING OR FIGHTING OR SWIMMING DURING CLASS HOURS, 'CAUSE I REALLY DON'T CARE.

EVIL 305. CURSES & DEATH TRAPS: NEMESIS DREAM
ANALYSIS
DEAN SOPHIE

"Know Your Enemy"—that is the key skill to surviving any fairy tale. By reading various primary texts that offer firsthand accounts of Nemesis Dreams (including mine!), you'll get insight into how a villain's unique soul conjures the symptoms of his or her future rival.

EVIL 306. CURSES & DEATH TRAPS: PHANTOM DUELS
DEAN SOPHIE

Limited to 8 Girls and 8 Boys—an intensive workshop in battling phantoms that replicate your future Good enemies, including princesses, princes, hunters, wily children, cuddly animals, and more.

EVIL 307. HISTORY SEMINAR: HISTORY OF WAR
PROFESSOR HORT

(See Good 310.)

EVIL 308. EVER KINGDOMS: PILLAGING & PILFERING
PROFESSOR SHEEKS

A thorough investigation of Ever kingdoms, including easily accessed entry points, trade routes vulnerable to sabotage, and current leadership structure (complete with illegally obtained gossip).

EVIL 309. ADVANCED SPELL CASTING: FLYING
PROFESSOR SHEEKS

This is our most advanced Evil seminar, which will teach our best Nevers how to soar through the air by relying on the power of their own bodies and the most sophisticated enchantments. (AND NO, WE DO NOT USE BROOMS.) Limited to 5 students only, chosen by a vote of the entire Evil faculty.

EVERS & NEVERS

GOOD 312/EVIL 310. SURVIVING FAIRY TALES
VARIOUS FOREST GROUP LEADERS

In the third-year course, students will travel the Woods each afternoon *without* Forest Group Leaders, creating their own curriculum of challenges in order to learn their unique limitations and the importance of protecting one another, both Evers and Nevers.

Year Four

In the fourth year of school, Evers and Nevers are formally divided into teams of Leaders, Helpers, and Mogrifs and assigned a specific yearlong quest in the Endless Woods. In the past, these quests have included:

★ Journeying to Drupathi and rescuing the imprisoned Princess of Maidenvale **(GOOD)**

★ Deep-diving to the remains of the *Jolly Roger* and searching for black-swan gold **(EVIL)**

★ Performing a civil audit of the accounts of Camelot after reports of corruption amongst the advisory council **(GOOD)**

★ Rebuilding and protecting the Gingerbread House, given a recent spate of plundering children **(EVIL)**

★ Writing and publishing a comprehensive biography of the Sader family **(GOOD & EVIL STUDENTS WITH A FOCUS ON HISTORY)**

★ Opening a trade outpost in Merlin's newly discovered kingdoms beyond the Shazabah Desert **(GOOD)**

★ Deposing the new, Good-sympathizing King of the Murmuring Mountains **(EVIL)**

At the end of the year, teams return to the School for Good and Evil to present the tales of their journeys in an elaborate graduation ceremony that is open to parents, friends, and past alumni.

From the Faculty

To help prepare you for the School for Good and Evil's rigorous curriculum, we have assembled some selections from the course work and reading that you may encounter during your first-year classes. We hope that this early preview will inspire you to attack your assignments with the dedication and enthusiasm that we expect from all our students.

From WINNING YOUR PRINCE
by Emma Anemone

Never underestimate the power of your own facial expressions. You must be constantly aware of what every muscle above your neck is doing. While a dazzling smile can lead a kingdom to hope and prosperity, an unintentional grimace can cause the *death* and *dismemberment* of millions of innocent soldiers. Indeed, this happened the night Queen Rania of Jaunt Jolie was meant to marry the Sultan of Shazabah

Match the Uglification spell or potion to the body part it most directly affects.

1. Bathing in raptor spit
2. "Vicious gubbalicious"
3. Drinking tadpole juice
4. Swallowing twelve rankleberries
5. "Cree crappolo prosciutto!"
6. Dousing the scalp with hornet milk

a. Face
b. Toenails
c. Elbow
d. Abdomen
e. Eyebrows
f. Hips

GOOD DEEDS Final Exa
Choose one of the followi
scenarios and write a
500-word essay:

1) You're sitting on your balcony swing sipping tea, and you notice a peacock wi a broken leg limping along a busy street. He's in danger b he's outside the castle walls, and your mother has strictly forbidden you from leaving the premises. What do you do

2) You're lost and starving in the Woods, and you find a cottage. There is a large feast on the table inside, but nobody is home. What do you do?

HISTORY OF VILLAINY MIDTERM QUIZ:

(Fill in the appropriate villain's name)

1) _____ killed Princess Anatole, who was known for her love of bears.

2) The witch who haunted fairies' dreams and convinced them to cut off their own wings was called _____ the _____ Eater.

3) The _____ Witch wore a bracelet made of little boys' bones.

4) The _____ of _____ was the Nemesis of Maid Marian's true love.

From THE RECIPE BOOK FOR GOOD LOOKS ⊙ *by Sedna Overcoat*

DIMPLE-MAKING WONTONS

(for those of us who weren't blessed with indented cheeks)

INGREDIENTS:

1 bolt of Pifflepaff Hills raw silk
2 teaspoons rainbow glitter
5 cubes skin-shrinking sugar
1 raven's egg

DIRECTIONS:

Cut the silk into 1-inch squares. Stir together glitter, sugar, and egg over a flame until the mixture starts to bubble. After it has cooled, take teaspoon-size portions and drop them onto the silken squares. Fold the silk over the filling and tie the corners into knots. Freeze for at least 10 days before eating.

From the chapter "Wintertime Spells"
from SPELLS FOR SUFFERING
by Angus the Giant

. . To turn your Nemesis into a snowman, you must first place your hand in a bucket of ice. Once the tips—and only the tips—of your fingers turn blue, channel your fingerglow and conjure the image of a whirling tornado of icicles and rocks—and then point your left pinkie at said enemy. If you end up feeling sorry for your Nemesis and want to reverse this spell, you might want to try reading A Ninny's Guide to Stupid and Cowardly Things (I can't fully remember the title, but it was something like that).

As if reading textbooks and acing a few tests is going to help you survive this place. Pfft! Here's what you really need to know, Nevers. (Evers, I'm giving you secrets from the enemy. Pay attention.)

HOW TO BE THE MOST RESPECTED VILLAIN IN SCHOOL BY HESTER

1.   On the first day, identify a spineless, stupid classmate (probably a Reader). Promise to protect him/her in exchange for being your loyal henchman for the next three years. Publicly command your henchman to fetch your lunch, carry your books, and spread rumors about the princesses you killed before you started school, and watch your classmates' respect grow.

2.   Target the most handsome, popular Everboy and come up with an appropriately wimpy nickname for him (e.g., Glitterbreath, Nancypants, Strawberry Kisses). Make sure all the other Nevers only call him by that name. His pride will eventually crumble, and victory will be yours.

FLUFFY BREECHES!

3. Learn one dangerous, unapproved spell from the books in the Library of Vice. Use this spell on your worst enemy (Ever or Never) in an appropriately public setting. It will get you sent to the Doom Room, but you will earn everlasting fear and respect. (Note: See "How to Survive the Doom Room" page 50.)

4. Never, ever let anyone see you use the toilet. A villain loses all menace and credibility once he or she is seen doing something so hideously normal. You are above this.

5. At least once a week, deliberately sleep somewhere other than your own dorm room (my favorite spots: the Belfry, the hallway outside the Library of Vice, behind the sofa in the Mischief Common Room). The next morning, walk into class with a bloodstained uniform. Your roommates will spread rumors about your sinister nighttime escapades, and it will enhance your mystique.

6. Study and put in the hard work to be number 1 in the Evil rankings. This might affect your social life but will make you feared and respected. If another student surpasses you, then "accidentally" attack your rival during a class challenge. They will get the point.

The School for Good and Evil
CAREER COUNSELING OFFICE

After your first year as a student at the School for Good and Evil, you will have the opportunity to apply for an internship or a study-abroad program at one of the many unique kingdoms scattered throughout the Endless Woods. Here is a sampling of just some of the opportunities available to our students. Bear in mind that if you are ranked in the lower third of your class, you will be required to take remedial summer classes with Castor, who gets very grumpy about having to work during the off-season.

Kindly,

Vivian Shoemaker

Vivian Shoemaker
Internship Coordinator

Study-Abroad Programs

EVERS

LEADERSHIP TRAINING IN CAMELOT
HOST: AGATHA AND TEDROS OF CAMELOT

Learn what it takes to run a historic kingdom from two of SGE's most celebrated alumni. Participants in this program will see firsthand how Agatha and Tedros, Camelot's newest rulers, balance the royal coffers, overhaul the health care system, negotiate beneficial relationships with allied kingdoms, and figure out how to get the kingdom's septic system up and running because they are quickly running out of buckets. To apply to this program, Evers must write a research paper about the political history of Camelot. Only 2 students will be selected.

FEMINISM INTENSIVE IN MAIDENVALE
HOST: BRIAR ROSE OF MAIDENVALE &
JACK OF WOODS BEYOND

Before her death, Ella personally selected Briar Rose and Jack to inaugurate and run the Maidenvale Feminist Research Center. Participants in this program will help the new cochairs develop the center's schedule and curriculum, manage outreach initiatives, and keep away any empty-headed pig princes who do not ascribe to the MFRC cause. To apply, a student must submit an essay about his or her most respected feminist icon.

THE HISTORY OF YOUTH CULTURE IN NEVERLAND
HOST: PETER PAN

Yes, Evergirls and -boys, we all get old, even if we don't think we're going to. However, even if our skin is wrinkled and we feel like our bones are made of dry twigs, that doesn't mean we can't be young at heart. Spend your summer months exploring the Lost Boys' hangout, the Mermaids' Lagoon, Tiger Lily's home, and the rest of the memorable sites from Peter Pan's fairy tale. This program is intended to help more serious-minded students get a break from the stress of schoolwork and societal expectations. There's no application process—just show up with a signed permission slip from your parents and maybe some gash-healing salve.

SCOUTING THE ENDLESS WOODS
HOST: THE GILLIKIN FAIRIES

At least a third of you will end up tracked as sidekicks, which means that you will have to be sharply attuned to all the pathways and deadly traps hidden throughout our Woods. Who better to teach you than a pack of the most experienced Gillikin fairies—an Ever's best friend when navigating the Woods. You will scout every corner of the forest and learn useful skills in survival, map reading, astrology, orienteering, bushwhacking, scrounging, and identifying different types of vegetation. This program is not for the weak of heart or the weak of stomach (wild berries can be rough on the digestive system). Successful completion of a 30-minute obstacle course is necessary for acceptance.

NEVERS

HUNTING FOR SWAMP THINGS IN THE BOGLANDS
HOST: WANDA THE WITCH, LOCAL ENTREPRENEUR

What better way to spend your summer than mucking through the muddy Boglands? Follow longtime resident Wanda the Witch on her daily treks through the swamp to collect materials and creatures for her workshop. This program is perfect for students who like dirt, mud, slugs, manure, mucus, and humidity and aren't afraid of scorpion bites. You will live with Wanda in her authentic Boglands thatch hut and eat the local cuisine, which consists primarily of dirt, mud, slugs, manure, mucus, and sometimes bugs. This will be an eye-opening cultural experience for Nevers facing a sticky, sweaty future.

EVIL ECONOMICS INDEPENDENT STUDY IN FOXWOOD
HOST: CAPTAIN VERNON BULLDOG, CEO, SMEE & SONS NEW-AND-IMPROVED BOOTY AUCTION

"You put a price on things and then you sell them to people who want them," says Woods-renowned businessman Captain Vernon Bulldog, who recently took over this famous high-end marketplace for stolen treasure. Participants in this program will become experts in rejecting silly "morals" and "values" when it comes to getting rich, based on Bulldog's philosophy that "people die but gold doesn't." Applicants need to relay a story about a time when they prioritized material things over a family member.

INVESTIGATING THE MOB MENTALITY IN HAMELIN

HOST: JONAH OF HAMELIN, AKA THE PIED PIPER

What makes a group of children follow a man with a flute who can usually only attract a rat's attention? Why would a well-established institution suddenly abandon coeducational education and split into two groups that eventually go to war? Led by Jonah of Hamelin, students will engage in serious debates and discussions about what influences large groups of people, animals, and other living creatures to act in certain ways. In addition, you will learn large-scale choreographed dances, popular uprising chants, and boot camp exercises to understand the mob mind-set. This program is specifically geared towards students who lack individuality, follow trends without thinking about it, and can't do anything without a friend.

THE ART OF HARVESTING KILLER WEEDS IN MAHADEVA

HOST: KRISCILLA, THE EVIL QUEEN OF THE NORTHWEST

Can't tell the difference between a man-eating hill and a vegetarian one? Then come to Mahadeva this summer. Get out your most flexible armor and your scythe, and prepare to learn everything you need to know about killing your enemies with just a simple plant. This program combines chemistry, sorcery, botany, and methodology for sneaking deadly potions into a beverage without the knowledge of your Nemesis. Please understand that Queen Kriscilla has many royal duties, and students will only be allowed a brief audience with her once a week—her army of evil minions will run the bulk of the curriculum. However, accepted students will have the opportunity to work and live in the queen's luxurious haunted castle and wander its deadly grounds, hidden deep in the Mahadeva Hills.

Internships

EVERS

ALTAZARRA UNICORN FARM

Altazarra Unicorn Farm, *the* most elite provider of unicorn hair in the Endless Woods, is looking for 2 student interns. Their responsibilities will include brushing the unicorns, braiding the unicorns' hair, singing to the unicorns, bathing the unicorns in honeycream, reading poetry to the unicorns, maintaining the unicorns' self-esteem, making the unicorns' beds, cleaning the unicorns' lap-pool, and blending fresh-fruit smoothies for the unicorns, amongst other things. To be considered, please send a charcoal drawing of yourself with a unicorn as well as an essay about why you love these ethereal creatures.

THE WHITE RABBIT'S CLOCK-MAKING FACTORY

Did you know that most of the enchanted timepieces in the Woods come from one place? Yes, that's right—the White Rabbit's Clock-Making Factory is the source for *all* your time-telling needs. We would like to hire an intern who is interested in tinkering, fidgeting, building, constructing, assembling, and manufacturing alongside our award-winning watchmakers and technicians. The intern would also be responsible for keeping all the interfactory clocks perfectly synced, calling lunch hours and teatimes, and making sure our CEO, the White Rabbit, is never late for anything. Applicants must deliver a completed form and a handmade time-telling device to our Malabar Hills office by exactly 12:41:08 p.m. on September 23.

GEPPETTO'S WORKSHOP

Geppetto's Workshop has been hiring interns from the School for Good and Evil for many years, and we are pleased to say that so far, everyone has had a great experience! Interns must have an excellent knowledge of human, Mogrif, fairy, and troll anatomy, as they will be assisting our designers while they sketch and lay out the wooden pieces that make up our high-quality, one-of-a-kind wooden figures and body parts. Interns must also be well versed in first aid, as slips of the saw are sadly quite common. Prospective applicants need to come to the workshop for an in-person interview and demonstrate the ability to tell the difference between puppets and real people.

CINDERELLA'S MICE DESIGNS, LTD.

For those Evergirls and Everboys who have an interest in fashion, Cinderella's Mice Designs, Ltd., in Maidenvale is looking for an intern. He or she will be responsible for helping the founders keep up with their correspondence (as it is difficult for mice to hold quills), recruiting models from around the Woods, and assisting our coordinators to stage the company's fashion shows every season. Our intern *must* be chic, stylish, suave, and confident—but not too confident to make morning tea for everyone.

NEVERS

NETHERWOOD VILLAIN DIGEST

Interested in bringing down your enemy . . . in print? Come intern for the *Netherwood Villain Digest*. You will get to work under famed editor-in-chief Karishma Tarantula and learn all the ins and outs of evil journalism. As an intern, you will learn how to go undercover and dig out the most scandalous and eyebrow-raising stories. However, if you fail at that, you're of no use to us and will likely spend most of your internship picking cobwebs out from between Lumpy Lou (our night editor)'s fingers and toes. Applicants must prove that they have a brain, a spine, and a very tiny heart.

NECRO RIDGE

we need help digging graves but we can't pay you and Dean Sophie said we could have free labor if we called them interns so please come help we are very behind in our schedule and too many dead bodies festering

JESTER'S JINX SHOP

Hey hey hey, all you clowns and tricksters out there! Do you want to learn how to prank with the best of them? Then come be our intern at Jester's Jinx Shop in Nettle Forest! You will get to work at the front desk, help with our mail-order business, and test out new products! Other intern activities include knitting scarves with your teeth, making cupcakes out of only air and dirt, and figuring out how to stop the rain on gloomy days. Only one of those things is true! Ha-ha! Send us a list of your best jokes in order to be considered.

EVIL LINGUISTICS SOCIETY

Dead languages are one of the great tragedies of our times, and the Evil Linguistics Society in Roch Briar has dedicated the last 50 years to unearthing them. As an intern, you will assist our translators as they retrieve deadly curses and chants from ancient tomes (and do your best not to get those books dirty or we'll bury you underneath a pile of them). You will gain some insight into the ancient history of Evil. Also, we promise to teach you curse words in other languages so you can insult your classmates without getting in trouble. Applicants, get excited to spend 3 months in a dingy basement library with no heat! Please send us a book of matches with your application form, as we are running dangerously short and it's so dark down here . . . almost too dark, even for all us villains.

THE SCHOOL FOR GOOD AND EVIL

Revamped First-Year Academic Calendar

November 11	New Students Arrival & Welcoming
November 12	Textbook & Uniform Distribution
November 13	First Day of Classes; Ever-Never Challenge begins
December 15	Trial by Tale (Fall)
December 26–January 3	Winter Holiday
January 6–13	Annual Sidekick Challenge
February 13	The Circus of Talents
February 14	The Evers Snow Ball (or the Nevers No Ball)
March 1–3	Parents' Visiting Weekend

March 10	First-Year Field Trip to Garden of Good and Evil
March 17–24	School Musical (open to public)
March 28	Trial by Tale (Spring)
April 2	Fairy and Wolf Appreciation Day
April 10	Leonora Lesso Memorial Day (no school)
April 15–22	Ever-Never Color War & Spirit Week
May 1	Deadline for Study-Abroad Applications for Year 2
May 15	Last Day of Ever-Never Challenge
May 16	Winning School Announced
May 17–May 23	Review for Finals
May 25–June 3	Final Exams and Practicals
June 4–August 25	Summer Session and Mandatory Internships
September 6	Year 2 Classes Begin

Parents'

We at the School for Good and Evil look forward to welcoming your families every year, many of whose members are illustrious alumni themselves. Because of the previous School Master's nasty habit of kidnapping Readers, it would have been rather awkward to extend the invitation to Reader families in the past, but this year, we hope that some will attend! In the meantime, please enjoy a few precious moments from the past. . . .

Aladdin of Shazabah returning to visit his grandson, Kaveen, during his first year at the School for Good.

The Sheriff of Nottingham and his lovely wife, Patricia, practicing archery with their daughter, Dot.

Weekend

Briar Rose and Prince Robert listen to granddaughter Millicent reading a story at the school literary festival.

The Wicked Witch of the West (formerly Griselda of Ravenbow) takes time off from her busy schedule to spend some quality time with her daughter, Mona of Oz, in her dormitory.

Health & Wellness

LUNCHTIME LECTURES

By DEAN SOPHIE

All Evers and Nevers are invited to attend Dean Sophie's famous lecture series every Friday in the Clearing during lunchtime. As a preview of this year's curriculum, we offer you a selection of her most helpful tips!

If you have dry hair . . . you can massage some coconut oil into your scalp, but not too much. Can you imagine what would have happened if Rapunzel's braid had been slick and greasy? "Rapunzel, Rapunzel, let down your—" SPLAT.

If your skin is a bit overwrought . . . you can mix up some sandalwood powder, lemon rind, and honeysuckle extract and rub the paste all over your face. After twenty minutes, your visage will be as smooth as a porcelain doll's. This will not, however, cure those of you with naturally sour, gloomy, or repellent expressions.

If you want to get rid of some unsightly hairs . . . you can create a homemade wax out of ground sugarcane, honey, and juniper oil (also useful for ripping off your enemy's eyebrow while he sleeps).

If your armpits emit an unpleasant odor . . . you can make a spritz out of gardenia buds, dried rosemary, and apple cider. This will not help those Nevers whose entire diet consists of garlic-flavored pigs' feet or those princes who down twelve raw eggs a day trying to get buff.

If your bottom jiggles like a cherry pudding when you walk . . . you can put one leg in front of the other with your hands on your hips and lower yourself to the ground at least two hundred times each morning. To keep motivated, recruit a friend to prod you with a sharpened twig throughout.

If your teeth are an unfortunate shade of mustard . . . you can prepare your own whitening paste using sea salt, ground parsley seeds, and diamond-flecked fairy clay from the caves of Foxwood, which, I assure you, is a worthy investment, even if it puts you into a lifetime of debt.

If your best friend is delinquent in answering your correspondence . . . and it seems clear that she doesn't find you as interesting as some boorish, sword-toting man-child . . . then perhaps it is time to send her a velvet pouch lined with porcupine quills and dried snake urine.

Schedule of LUNCHTIME LECTURES

LUNCHTIME with SOPHIE

ARCHIVAL SERIES:

Topic: Black Is the New Black

Friday, November 13

LUNCHTIME with SOPHIE

ARCHIVAL SERIES:

Topic: Malevolent Makeovers

Friday, December 11

LUNCHTIME with SOPHIE

INTERNAL SELF-BETTERMENT SERIES:

Topic: Wearing Scars with Confidence

Friday, November 20

LUNCHTIME with SOPHIE

ARCHIVAL SERIES:

Topic: Abandon All Ye Clumps!

Friday, December 18

LUNCHTIME with SOPHIE

READER INTEGRATION SERIES:

Topic: How to Speak Sensitively to Your Horned Classmates

Friday, November 27

LUNCHTIME with SOPHIE

INTERNAL SELF-BETTERMENT SERIES:

Topic: Learning to Deal with the Pain of Wearing Heels

Friday, December 25

LUNCHTIME with SOPHIE

READER INTEGRATION SERIES:

Topic: Reader/Descendant Relationships

Friday, December 4

LUNCHTIME with SOPHIE

INTERNAL SELF-BETTERMENT SERIES:

Topic: Using Gems to Heal a Broken Heart

Friday, January 8

Dear Ever or Never,

Health and wellness at the School for Good and Evil is
not just about beauty, no matter what anyone may preach
(at lunchtime or otherwise). Instead, health and wellness
are about knowing you belong here and that whatever
happens, you will find your destiny, whether as a Leader,
a Helper, or a Mogrif. All three are crucial in every fairy
tale—imagine Tedros' story without Merlin, for instance,
or Agatha's story without Wish Fish! Neither Merlin nor
those fish were tracked as Leaders during their time at school,
but they understood that they served a greater role in the
Endless Woods beyond themselves.

In the next pages, we offer you a chance to see how you
might perform both at school and in the Endless Woods
upon graduation, just a few short years from now.

Happy Testing!

Clarissa Dovey
Clarissa Dovey

P.S. Dean Sophie insisted on including one of her own
quizzes. Consider it strictly optional.

(FOR EVERS)

WHAT DOES YOUR FUTURE HOLD?
By Dean Clarissa Dovey

1) What is the best way to describe the way you felt upon arriving at the School for Good and Evil?
   a. Nervous but ready for the challenges ahead
   b. Excited to make so many new friends
   c. Ready to turn around and go right back home
   d. Filled with anger and rage

2) Which of the following items was the first thing you unpacked from your trunk upon arrival?
   a. A copy of A *Student's History of the Woods* by August A. Sader
   b. An address book filled with the contact information of all your friends from home
   c. A pair of rubber slippers to protect your feet from fungus in the dormitory showers
   d. A hatchet and accompanying hatchet-sharpener (which, by the way, are not approved!)

3) When you were a child, what was your favorite fairy tale?
   a. *Cinderella*—because love and goodness win in the end
   b. *Sleeping Beauty*—because the fairies were such wonderful friends to Briar Rose
   c. *Little Red Riding Hood*—because she had the best snacks
   d. *Children Noodle Soup*—because children are horrible, but so tasty in consommé

4) Which extracurricular activities are you most excited to pursue at school?
   a. The SGE Student Council—so you can make a real difference in your community
   b. The SGE Slumber Party Club—so you can get to know your classmates better!
   c. The (Unapproved and Unofficial) SGE Nap Society— because you can't be bothered to participate in extracurricular activities
   d. The SGE Evil Entrepreneur Association—because collaboration is vital to Evil world domination.

5) In which part of the School for Good and Evil do you anticipate spending the most time?
   a. The Library (of Virtue *or* Vice)
   b. The Dormitories
   c. The Supper Hall
   d. The Doom Room

Tally up your answers!

If you answered mostly "a"—You're on your way to being a Leader! You are coming into school ready to learn, work hard, and face the obstacles and victories that await you over the next four years.

If you answered mostly "b"—You have the personality to become a devoted Helper. You love being around people and soaking up everything your teachers and classmates have to offer.

If you answered mostly "c"—You're not very motivated, are you? I anticipate having to discipline you a fair bit and warn you frequently that you're on the verge of failing. If you do manage to make it through all four years, I think you're very likely to become a Mogrif. Don't be too dejected, though—Mogrifs are just as vital to fairy tales as princes and princesses!

If you answered mostly "d"—You already have the stirrings of darkness inside you, so you are likely going to end up under the jurisdiction of Dean Sophie in the School for Evil. I hope you become a worthy adversary for my students.

Self-Quiz for Self-Assessment #2

(FOR EVERS)

HOW LONG WILL YOU SURVIVE IN THE WOODS?
By Princess Uma

1) You're lost in the Woods, it's getting dark, and your last match just went out. What do you do?
    a. Sing a charming melody in the hopes that an animal friend comes to your rescue
    b. Start a fire with flint and a knife
    c. Curl up in a little ball and weep until the sun rises
    d. Just reading this sentence made my stomach turn inside out. I want to go home!

2) Which of the following animals is best to consult if you're uncertain whether a berry is poisonous or not?
    a. A sweet-tempered chickadee
    b. A wise turtle
    c. A lazy sloth
    d. I'd rather starve than take a chance.

3) What is the best place to hide from a hailstorm?
    a. Underneath the wings of a passing falcon
    b. Beneath an umbrella woven out of gronkonia leaves and thick butter-reeds
    c. Curled up in a little ball and weeping until it passes
    d. What's a hailstorm? Does it hurt? *Mommyyyy!*

4) How do you best protect your feet from crog spines on the forest floor?

   a. I'm not worried—crogs are usually pretty good at cleaning up after themselves.
   b. By coating my shoe soles in a thick layer of beetle shellac
   c. Pray really hard that my entire journey will take place on soft moss
   d. Don't go into the forest, obviously!

5) Which of the following tactics best repels death sparrows?

   a. I'm not sure how to repel them, but extract from the leaves of the ylang-ylang tree can calm down even the meanest of creatures.
   b. Digging a hole in the ground, filling it with dried ragebrush, and lighting it on fire
   c. Digging a hole in the ground and hiding in it
   d. Begging for mercy?

Tally up your answers!

If you answered mostly "a"—You are a very gracious and warmhearted person! Still, you may be a little *too* nice and trusting to survive more than a week or two in the Woods. We'll have to toughen you up!

If you answered mostly "b"—Bravo! You already have the makings of an excellent woodsman or woods-woman and will last in the Woods for as long as you need!

If you answered mostly "c"—Oh dear. We will have to work on your courage now, won't we? Don't worry, we *definitely* will not be sending you into the Woods until you're ready (however long it takes).

If you answered mostly "d"—Um . . . every teacher loves a challenge?

Self-Quiz for Self-Assessment #3

(FOR NEVERS)

VILLAIN OR HENCHMAN?
By Castor

1. If you're in the Woods and you see a wee little Evergirl lost and crying, do you:
   a. Get her to shut up and then eat her (after dousing her in hairinara sauce).
   b. Ask your fellow travelers to deal with it so it's not your problem.
   c. Pretend you don't see her and go eat a sandwich instead.
   d. Wipe the snot off her face and help her find her way home.

2. During a bloody battle between Good and Evil, do you:
   a. Rip the Good Army to pieces single-handedly and then enjoy a hearty lunch.
   b. Fight next to the Evil Leader and pray that you don't die.
   c. Stand at the back of the army and swing your sword around in the air.
   d. Play dead three miles away from the battlefield until everything blows over.

3. When hanging out with your Evil friends, do you:
   a. Draft plans to conquer the world and wipe out Good forever.
   b. Listen to your best friend draft plans to conquer the world and wipe out Good forever.
   c. Refill everyone's cups and snack bowls.
   d. Friends? Where?! I'm so lonely.

4. Evil is organizing a rugby team to play against Good's. What position do you sign up for?
   a. The captain: the leader of the team who makes the key decisions
   b. The forwards, or the strongest players who lead the charge towards the goal
   c. The backs, or the last line of defense
   d. I'm allergic to contact sports.

5. During the annual Sidekick Challenge, how would you tame your sidekick?
   a. I won't need to. Everyone in the Woods knows to obey my orders.
   b. Lock it in the Ever's Groom Room until its spirit breaks.
   c. Pet it like a bunny and dress it in a little raincoat.
   d. Summon my mother to come and take care of it because the stress makes me constipated.

Tally up your answers!

If you answered mostly "a"—VILLAIN! EVERS AND NEVERS ALIKE WILL SHIVER WHEN THEY HEAR YOUR NAME.

If you answered mostly "b"—YOU'RE A HENCHMAN WHO WILL SPEND YOUR LIFE STUCK TO YOUR LEADER'S BEHIND LIKE A BARNACLE ON A PIRATE SHIP.

If you answered mostly "c"—YOU'LL MAKE A GOOD MOGRIFIED ANIMAL, LOCKED IN A CAGE EVERY NIGHT AND FORCED TO EAT SCRAPS OFF THE FLOOR.

If you answered mostly "d"—YOU'RE GONNA END UP A TREE. LOOK AT YOUR ANSWERS. YOU SOUND EXACTLY LIKE A TREE!

(FOR ANYONE WHO BELIEVES
IN LIVING A FULFILLED LIFE)

WHAT IS YOUR BEAUTY PROFILE?
By Dean Sophie

1) When you first wake up in the morning, you . . .
   a. Brush your teeth and splash warm water on your face.
   b. Eat a hearty breakfast.
   c. Chew on rocks and roll around on the stable floor.
   d. Use cleanser, serum, toner, moisturizer, face mist, body oil, and skin mask, followed by yoga, makeup application, hairstyling, and dressing with the assistance of a highly trained chambermaid.

2) Which of the following best describes the way you feel about going to a ball?
   a. I enjoy a good formal party a few times a year.
   b. I'll go, I suppose, but I'd rather read a book.
   c. If you try to make me attend a ball, I will empty you of all your organs.
   d. Seeing as a ball is not truly a ball without my stunning, regal presence, I see my attendance as a gift to humanity.

3) What is your closet mostly filled with?
   a. Smart-looking, practical clothing and shoes, with a few special outfits for big events
   b. Black tunics, clumps, and torn stockings
   c. Crates of manure, slingshots to fling said manure at others, unwashed underpants, and several jars of junglefish eyeballs preserved in vinegar

d. Eighteen custom-made gowns by Madame Clotilde van Zarachin, winner of the Gold Award from the Council of Fashion Designers of Everwood, as well as dozens of glass slippers with gemstone embellishments and six tailored cashmere and velvet-lined coats

4) What is the best time of year to harvest slugs?
   a. I've never harvested slugs because I'm a little squeamish, but logic tells me that they're likely to be roaming around when it's hot and muggy outside.
   b. I often collect slugs for my experiments, and I know that the best time to get them is during the rainy season.
   c. I didn't hear the question because I have a parade of slugs coming out of my ears.
   d. You've got to be kidding. Ask the gardener.

5) What is your favorite scent?
   a. I love anything light and clean—like fresh orange blossoms.
   b. I prefer my natural scent, even if I haven't bathed in a few days.
   c. Whatever comes from rolling around in the stables
   d. A dusting of frangipani-laced talcum powder right out of the bath and then a dab of lavender, patchouli, and vanilla at all my pulse points

---

Tally up your answers!

If you answered mostly "a"—It's a good thing you met me! You may have a basic understanding of hygiene for now, but without my intervention, your beauty will start to fade *much* sooner than you expect.

If you answered mostly "b"—Agatha? Is that you? Get thee to the Groom Room *immediately*.

If you answered mostly "c"—I advise you to smash all the mirrors in your dorm room, lock yourself in a closet, and swallow the key.

If you answered mostly "d"—There are only two ways you got this score. Either you're lying or you're me.

School Musical

Curses!
The School Musical

Director's Note:

How can there be a school without a school show? Every place of education needs an annual exhibition of its values, its traditions, its *taste*. For a school of such size and legendary significance to still be standing without ever having put on a poetry reading, let alone a dramatic production . . . it's not only an embarrassment but a crime. Needless to say, my first act as Dean was to add a substantial budget for a yearly musical of the highest dramatic and aesthetic standards.

As to what our first show would be, where else could we start but with my own story? Ideally it would be a one-woman extravaganza, mixing burlesque, Kabuki, and Sturm und Drang, which I would write, star in, produce, direct, and compose . . . but Dean Dovey seemed a bit put out by the idea. And I do admit, it would defeat the purpose of having a school musical if I was the only one in it.

At which point, I remembered I had an old script gathering dust that told the story of Agatha's and my adventures at the School for Good and Evil . . . a story as grand in its scale as in its emotions. . . . All it needed was a bit of revision, now that our tale finally has an ending.

As a point of policy, all Evers and Nevers are required to try out for the show, which is essential to preserving unity, spirit, and bonhomie between our two schools. (Those of you without a modicum of talent will be set builders, stage managers, or painted to look like trees.)

See you at auditions!

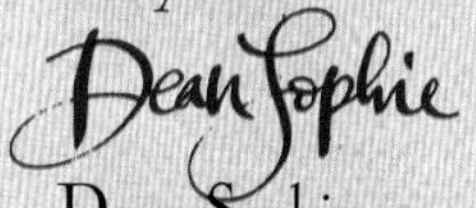

Dean Sophie

Dean Sophie

Curses!
The Musical

AUDITION SIDES

NOTE: *Please have all lines memorized in advance of your audition. You may audition by playing any part you choose (though we prefer boys play boys and girls play girls for the sake of simplicity).*

AUDITION SCENE 1: A quaint village called Gavaldon. Sophie and Agatha walk through a graveyard together.

SOPHIE: I've waited my whole life to be kidnapped.

AGATHA: Oh please, there is no School Master, and there is no school. And there definitely is no prince.

SOPHIE: Prince? I don't want a prince. Who needs some blond, muscled Adonis who will turn on you the moment he has a chance and run away with your best friend?

AGATHA: Don't look at me. I don't want a prince either.

SOPHIE: Oh-ho! You say that now. And what if I was to say you'll end up with one?

AGATHA: I would say that if there was, in fact, a version of me that ended up with a prince, she's an impostor.

SOPHIE: A nefarious, malingering, backstabbing impostor?

AGATHA: Um, sure. If I had anything to do with a prince, you could call me anything you want.

SOPHIE: Hmmm, I'll take you up on that. Maybe I'll sing a song about it. Oh dear, I believe a pigeon just pooed on your face. *(wipes away poo)*

AGATHA: Oh Sophie, you are not only beautiful and kind, but also a wonderful friend.

AUDITION SCENE 2: The Clearing at the School
for Good and Evil. Tedros and Sophie talk.

TEDROS: Look, I really want to marry you, Sophie, but I feel like
you can do better than me. You're so smart and pretty,
and I'm so dull and a cliché.

SOPHIE: You're right, Tedros. It's just hard to find someone as
beautiful as me, so I had to at least give you a chance.

TEDROS: And I appreciate you giving me a chance, even though
I am a fool. My life is better for knowing you. But the
truth is, I think the School Master has a crush on you.

SOPHIE: Isn't the School Master . . . *old*?

TEDROS: No, he's secretly young and perfect and looks like Jack
Frost.

SOPHIE (*gazing at the School Master in his window*):
I always wanted to kiss Jack Frost.

TEDROS: Just don't forget Tedros when you two are married.

SOPHIE (*still staring at the School Master*): Tedros who?

(*Tedros frowns. Agatha arrives with Hort.*)

AGATHA: Sophie, Hort wants me to set you two up. He found out
we're friends, and now he won't stop bothering me.

SOPHIE (*sighs*): Why are there so many boys in love with me?

HORT: Can I touch your hair? Or have some of it?

SOPHIE: Come back when you add fifty pounds of muscle and a
tan.

HORT: You promise you'll let me touch you then?

SOPHIE: Um. No promises. But at the very least, you'll be easier
to look at.

(*Hort bounds away. Kiko comes up.*)

KIKO: Agatha, I wanted to—

SOPHIE (*waves her away*): No autographs, please!

Curses!
The Musical

AUDITION SONG

DIRECTOR'S NOTE: *This song is one of the many Dean Sophie original compositions from* CURSES! THE MUSICAL. *It represents a crucial development in the arc of the Sophie character, testifying to the power of her emotional journey. All individuals auditioning must be able to sing it* IMPECCABLY.

"SOME GIRLS"
(*sung by* SOPHIE)

Some girls have pimples
Some girls have warts
Some girls have mermaid tails
Some can wear shorts.

Most girls have problems
To which we can all relate
But I've got an issue that
Really takes the cake. . . .

I've got too many boys running after me
I can't go anywhere
I just cannot be free
They're at my window when I wake up

They're slipping down my chimney at night
They're hiding under my bed and
They're getting into fights . . . over *me*!
And all I want is to be free. . . .

Some girls have bad teeth and
Some girls eat hair
Some girls are selfish and
Some girls can share.

All girls have problems
So many problems, it's true
But I promise that I'm
Much worse off than you . . . because . . .

I've got too many boys running after me
They won't leave me alone
I just cannot be free
They keep buying me gifts
And inviting me on dates
They have gotten past my guard dogs
And jumped over my gates . . .

But I've had enough
It's over, I say!
So all of you boys—just go away!

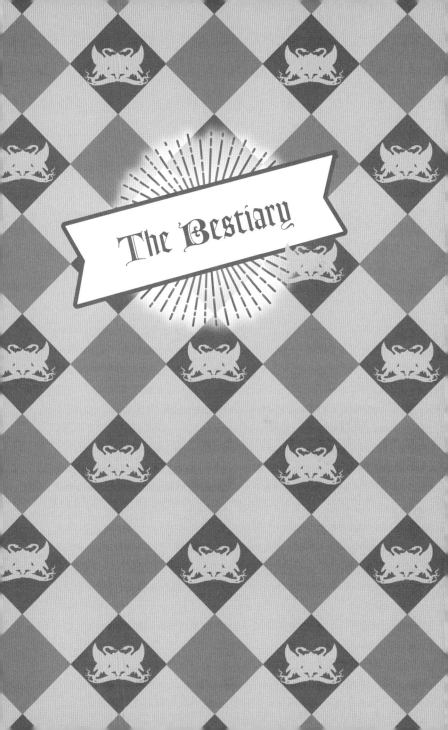

The Bestiary

INTRODUCTION

The previous School Master created the Blue Forest to keep the students at the School for Good and Evil safe from the lethal creatures that dwell in the Woods. However, during the end of his reign, chaos and impending war led some of these safeguards to crumble. While the nymphs, fairies, gargoyles, and wolves have done their best to repel deadly beasts from the castle, you might find one or two lingering about. Therefore, we have included a helpful diagram and some history to help students defend themselves in case of a surprise attack.

Friends of Good

Nymph

Hoverus protectus

Fairies
GLITTERUS OBEDIUS

Nymphs
(*Hoverus protectus*)

- Trained as security guards for the School for Good. Ironically, many nymphs have served as models for figureheads on pirate ships.
- Neon hair in various colors depending on strength and ranking within their colonies
- Extremely organized
- Power to levitate without wings
- Generally reach seven feet in height by the age of five

Fairies
(Glitterus obedius)

- Responsible for patrol and discipline at the School for Good
- Unmatched strength (can lift the weight of an adult man)
- Predisposed to sugar addiction
- Bite when provoked
- Spit sticky, glittery gold nets to ensnare prey (e.g., wayward students)
- Ongoing rivalry with the nymphs

Spirick
PRICKLUS GRUMPUS

Friends of Evil

Stymph
Wingus Skeletus

Crog
Willkillus Trespassus

Crogs
(Willkillus trespassus)

- ❖ The largest and most aggressive members of the *Swimmawolfae* family
- ❖ Normally found in squishy, unclean places near a shore where humans frequently roam (hence their frequent appearance around the Evil castle)
- ❖ Thin, rectangular snouts
- ❖ Sharp teeth that turn black in adulthood due to poor dental hygiene
- ❖ Extremely violent towards female humans
- ❖ Repelled by the scent of violets and/or freshly churned butter

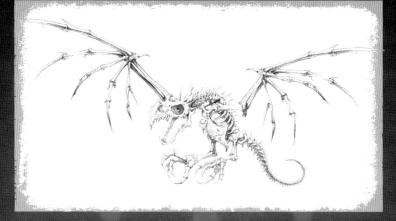

Stymphs
(*Wingus skeletus*)

- Large, winged creatures that tend to remain in one place for many generations
- Sleep within giant, black eggs surrounded by a yolky blanket
- Emit loud, ear-piercing shrieks when aroused from sleep after less than eight hours
- Despite hollow eye sockets, they maintain excellent nighttime vision.
- Protruding brow bones that are extremely sensitive to tickling
- Sharp, knifelike claws

Spiricks
(*Pricklus grumpus*)

- Tend to hide in wet, woody environments like piles of mulch or unattended saunas
- Acid-green eyes that light their way through dark swaths of forest
- Nest in groups of twenty to thirty, called "spirick circles"
- Surround their enemies and emanate a harmony of squeals before attacking
- Visibly take great joy in the suffering of others
- Sharpen their prickly exteriors by rubbing against trees—Mogrifs, beware.

Beyond the School

A Student's Guide to the Woods

Hello, young whippersnapper! Welcome to the Flowerground, the Woods' oldest public transportation system, which will ensure your safe passage between the School for Good and Evil and the many kingdoms that make up our world.

By way of introduction, I am Dante, the Conductor of the Flowerground. Here is a handy self-portrait so you'll recognize me when I demand to see your ticket:

Now, given the recent disciplinary incidents we've had on the Flowerground involving students of your school, I urge you to pay attention to this handy guide that will keep you healthy, happy, and *clothed* on your next journey. Remember: riding the flower-trains is a privilege and not a right.

HISTORY OF THE FLOWERGROUND

With the unfortunate passing of the last three history professors at the School for Good and Evil, I've asked your new history professor to explain how the Everwood Botanical Transit Authority came to be. He seemed reluctant, but I assured him it was tradition for the head of his department to regale students with the Flowerground's complex and colorful history in order to illuminate all the politics, negotiation, and diplomacy that went into the creation of the Woods' greatest public works.

WHERE TRAINS COME FROM
By Professor Hort of Bloodbrook

ONCE UPON A TIME, PEOPLE USED TO WALK IN THE ENDLESS WOODS. . . .

BUT ENDLESS WOODS ARE ENDLESS, SO THEY KEPT DISCOVERING NEW STUFF. . . .

SO THEN THEY TRIED RIDING HORSES LONG DISTANCES, BUT THAT DIDN'T WORK EITHER.

THE END

RULES OF RIDING

Admission & Fare

1.   The Flowerground is open only to Evers. Nevers who try to sneak in will be detected by our enchanted vines, thrown into burlap sacks, and beaten with carrot sticks before being ejected at the next stop. Nevers of the School for Good and Evil are allowed to ride at will, provided they are accompanied by a faculty member and are strapped into vine straitjackets that restrict nefarious movement. (Evers can ride unrestrained, as long as they have a Flowerground ticket.)

2.   However, Non-student Nevers are allowed to ride at will, provided they register at the Flowerground Registry Office, open on alternate Mondays from 3:00–3:30 p.m. If their registration is approved, they will be assigned a special EBTA (Everwood Botanical Transit Authority) Pre-Check Badge, which will let them ride the trains. (It will also facilitate full tracking of their movement and behavior, ensuring easy thwarting of any Evil schemes.)

3.   Flowerground tickets can only be purchased by visiting a local ticket office and presenting a suitable form of identification (such as birth certificate or illustrated storybook) containing your likeness. Local ticket offices serve all Everwood museums and

historical institutions, including: the *Jolly Roger*, Rapunzel's Tower, the Little Mermaid's Favorite Reef, and Bluebeard's Castle.

4. Single rides can be purchased for a small bag of vegetable, fruit, or flower seeds that can be used to replant the Flowerground. Monthly unlimited passes are available in exchange for three-ounce vials of liquefied gold.

5. The system is open twenty-four hours a day, but after 7:00 p.m., expect long delay times upon calling for a train.

Etiquette & Discipline

The code of behavior is simple:

NO SPITTING
NO SNEEZING
NO SINGING
NO SNIFFLING
NO SWINGING
NO SWEARING
NO SLAPPING
NO SLEEPING
NO URINATING

Violators will have all their clothes removed.

LEGEND

Hibiscus Line
Rosalinda Line
Tangerine Line
Arborea Line
Violet Line
Peony Line

Neverland

Jaunt Jolie

Gillikin

~~bow~~

Malabar Hills

Oakwood

Bloodbrook

Eternal Springs

Kingdom Kyrgios

Altazarra

Pasha Dunes

Flowerground Map

HIBISCUS

BRE		MURMURING ...NTAINS
7:3		
7:40		
7:50		
8:00	8:0	

ANADIL
c/o Dot's House
Sheriff's Office
Nottingham

HESTER
18 Rotten Peach Lane
(Gingerbread House)
Ravenswood

Hester,

Whatever you do, don't lose this letter. You always stuff your mail into books, and at this point, I'm sure you've littered your secrets across every library in the Endless Woods. Listen, I'm at Dot's house, and we have a serious problem. Sheriff finally knows where Robin Hood is and is sending his men out to kill him. But stupid Dot still has a crush on Robin! So now she's trying to sabotage her dad's attack, and if he finds out, he'll drown her in a well. You need to get here right now and help me

Hester darling,

Now don't go leaving this letter somewhere inappropriate like you always do! Sweetie, with the new class of students coming and all, I'm a bit anxious about what they'll think of me. I'd feel so much better if you were here for the Welcoming. Do you mind coming up and speaking at our Orientation? I'll make sure to send you private transportation by stymph and let you take any weapon you'd like from the Armory as payment, provided you don't tell Dovey. She really is a thorn in my rump

DEAN SOPHIE
c/o School for Good and Evil
Dean's Office
Evil Castle

HESTER
18 Rotten Peach Lane
(Gingerbread House)
Ravenswood

PEONY LINE

Kingdom Kyrgios	Eternal Springs	Bloodbrook
6:00	6:10	6:20
6:15	6:25	6:35
6:30	6:40	6:50
6:45	6:55	7:05
7:00	7:10	7:20
7:15	7:25	7:35
7:30	7:40	
7:45		
11:30		
11:45		
12:00		
12:15		
12:30		

DUNE

PIFFLEPAFF PUMPKIN
POINT

:30
:45
:00
:15
:30
:45
:00
:15
:30
:45
:00
:15
:30
:45
:00
:00

Dearest Hester,

First of all, relax. I've gotten every single one of your letters, including the last where you listed all the ways you'd murder me if I don't respond (#26 was especially creative). I haven't written back for a very good reason, and it's not because I'm "so fatheaded with power that I've forgotten my old friends" or "too busy smooching Tedros," as you put it.

I haven't forgotten anybody, Hester, least of all you. To be honest, I miss school terribly, and I would have traded my right foot to have been there those last six months and graduated with my friends—though it sounds like "Dean Sophie" nearly drove you and Anadil to stab yourselves by the end. Between those hideous new Never uniforms, mandatory lunchtime lectures, and ridiculous classes, I'm surprised you didn't snap and set your demon on Sophie in her sleep. (Did she really force all of you to be in a musical of THE TALE OF SOPHIE AND AGATHA? Send me the script immediately.)

But for all my secret wishes to be back at school, I figured out pretty quickly once we got to Camelot that I'm not a student anymore. First off, the castle was such a disaster— no food, no money, no functioning toilets—that we had to work night and day just to make the place presentable for Tedros' coronation. (He looked so handsome that I could see the drool on all the girls' faces. . . . I know how you feel about boys, so I'll stop here.) In any case, by the time I finally

:44
:50
:56
:02
:08
7:14
7:20
7:26
7:32
7:38
7:44
7:50
7:56
8:02
8:08
8:14
8:20
8:26
8:32
8:38
8:44
8:50
8:56

could write you, our pigeon courier had been eaten by the vultures circling the castle, so there was no way to even send my reply.

Speaking of vultures, there's plenty of the human kind trying to feast on what's left of King Arthur's kingdom. His council of advisers was supposed to rule in Tedros' place until Tedros was sixteen and instead took advantage of his absence to sneak money out of Camelot and into their pockets. Tedros had them thrown into the dungeons after his coronation, though one of the cretins has already escaped. (Lancelot is leading the search party.)

Luckily, I noticed Reaper had been tormenting this bat in the belfry, and I remembered from Animal Communication class that vultures hate bats . . . so now that cranky old beast is our new courier. (Cranky is an understatement: he delivers just one letter per flight, on whatever schedule he deems fit, and only in exchange for cucumbers and caviar. Sometimes I think it's Sophie in Mogrif form.)

On that note, I'm surprised that Sophie hasn't given you any news of Tedros and me. One of the reasons it took me so long to write you is that with the bat's one-letter rule, most of my notes have gone to Sophie (surprise, surprise). I know she's gotten them, because she's answered every last one. But if she hasn't mentioned our letters to each other, I shouldn't either. I don't want to be a bad friend.

That said, I have a hunch that Sophie and Tedros have been exchanging their own letters, because I caught him by the pool reading a pink card with her handwriting on it. He doesn't know I saw him, so I can't very well ask him about it. Plus, I don't tell him about Sophie's and my notes, so why should he tell me about his?

(Meanwhile, I think Tedros' mother has noticed they've been exchanging letters too. Whenever Merlin muses about having Sophie come to Camelot for a visit, Guinevere smiles but never goes so far as to extend an invitation.)

Speaking of mothers, I'm also relieved to hear you've forced yourself back into your mother's old gingerbread house, despite the frequent tour groups coming through. As you requested, I wrote a stern petition letter to the Everwood Architecture Society, asking them to restore its status as your private home. They wrote back that same night, saying that because I am not married to Tedros yet, my protest carries no weight and that the revenue from the tours of your mother's house far outweigh the inconvenience it is causing "an amateur witch." (It will not surprise you to know that Beatrix's mother runs the Everwood Architecture Society.)

But I suppose I'm avoiding your main question of how Tedros and I are getting on now that we're at Camelot. Oh, Hester ... where do I begin? First off, it's been uncomfortable between Tedros and me, because whenever we're alone, he keeps asking me to

8:48   8:5

INTERWOODS SOCIETY FOR TOURISM

Dear Student,

We at the InterWoods Society for Tourism are thrilled to hear that you have been accepted to the new first-year class at the School for Good and Evil.

For many years, we've had a strong relationship with your Deans in our effort to expose young minds to the incredible Ever and Never kingdoms that lie beyond your gates. Most of you, whether due to family duties or financial limitations, haven't had the opportunity to travel widely quite yet. But we encourage you to make trips (solo or with friends!) on your next holiday vacation, during your summer recess, and certainly during your fourth year. These trips can be not only pleasurable and educational, but also broaden your horizons as to where you might want to live after graduation.

To help you choose your next destination, we enclose a sample of postcards that will give you a sense of the many flavors of life that fill our wonderful Woods.

With all our best,

Bharthi Baswani

Liaison, InterWoods Society for Tourism

BLOODBROOK
OESN'T WANT
OUR KIND

Love from
NEVERLAND

RAVENBOW
where good people come to die

SEE WHAT'S UP IN
BORNA CORIC!

OFF
GDOM
RGIOS!

GRANDMOTHER'S HOUSE MUSEUM

Deep in Nettle Forest is a little old cottage where a little old lady and her granddaughter escaped certain death. Fifty years ago, Red Riding Hood (formerly Rita of Nettle Forest) decided to preserve her grandmother's hom and open it to the public. The mission of Grandmother's House Museum is to demonstrate the importance of home security to our visitors. It is an exciting, informative, and interactive experience for the whole family!

- Try to open state-of-the-art front door locks from all over the world! Bet you can't get them all!
- Dress up in fancy disguises and try to fool your friends! A portrait artist is available to capture the moment.
- Attempt to maneuver your way through an obstacle course and do your best to escape the booby traps!

- Take a carriage ride along the path that R herself took to Grandmother's house on fateful day—but all while trying to steer horse away from the placed trip wires!
- If you're tired and hungry, enjoy some biscuits and tea at the Kitchen Table Ca

WE ARE OPEN FROM 10:00 A.M. TO 4:00 P.M. EVERY DAY
COME VISIT US—IF YOU CAN GET INSIDE. OF COURSE.

THE RAPUNZEL MEMORIAL

"We'll be safe as long as we stick together," Rapunzel said to her beau, Prince Townsend, before they escaped from evil Mother Gothel. Little did she know that only ten short years later, Mother Gothel would return in zombie form to exact her revenge and kill them both.

This tower has stood in the center of Roch Briar since Rapunzel's fairy tale concluded. It used to be a bastion of hope, a symbol of joy, and a constant reminder that no matter how bleak the horizon may seem, a glimmer of sunshine will always find its way through. This year, we sadly have had to transform the museum at Rapunzel's Tower into a memorial that celebrates her brief life.

You can climb the steps to the room where Rapunzel was imprisoned and light a candle to place on the ledge. You can make a wish by throwing a coin from the roof into the glittering pond below. You can see the humble bed where Rapunzel lay every night during her years of captivity, now covered with a quilt that her two children sewed in her memory. Afterward, you can visit our gift shop and purchase a long blond braided wig or a soft plush vine toy. All proceeds go to the Everwood Society of Cultural Preservation.

$\mathcal{D}$o you have the guts to enter? This castle, erected over one thousand years ago, was once used to defend the Murmuring Mountains during the Great War. Bluebeard (formerly Drogan) inherited it from his grandfather soon after graduating from the School for Evil. He built his life there . . . and ended many others.

Bluebeard's Castle

Walk through the dungeon where the nefarious Bluebeard imprisoned and murdered his innumerable ex-wives.

- 💀 Hold the torture devices that Bluebeard himself used.
- 💀 See the key that opened the door to his dungeon and revealed Bluebeard's deadly secret.
- 💀 Ogle the wax cadavers of Bluebeard's victims.

Because of the somewhat uncomfortable nature of these exhibits, they are not recommended for children under the age of eight. Or anyone who faints easily, has a heart condition, or generally reacts poorly to images of suffering, torture, and death.

THE JOLLY ROGER
A DARK AND VILLAINOUS EXPERIENCE ON THE HIGH SEAS

$\mathcal{E}$xplore the dark and gloomy underbelly and the surprisingly pleasant deck of the most famous pirate ship in existence, now permanently docked off the coast of Neverland. (Sponsored by the Neverland Association for the Conservation of Pirate Booty)

- See Captain Hook's legendary collection of designer eye patches belonging to various pirates he vanquished.
- Notice the holes and dents resulting from ancient cannonballs.
- Enjoy a tour of the pirates' quarters, including the aromatherapy room that Smee built by hand to help the men relax.
- Meet (or rather see the taxidermic version of) Captain Hook's loyal parrot.
- Marvel at the preserved wooden legs, arms, and various other body parts of the Jolly Roger's original crew in our underwater exhibition.

The *Jolly Roger* is open daily from sunrise to sunset, and tours are offered every hour.

(*Anyone found trying to cause a mutiny amongst the volunteer staff will be swiftly removed from the premises.)

The Graduating Class

Dear Students,

In each new edition of the Ever Never Handbook, we pay an extended tribute to our most recent graduating class: those apprentices of Good and Evil who have survived three grueling years of school and are now pursuing their assigned quests in the fourth year.

Each of these quests is fraught with danger. But regardless of whether these former students succeed or fail in their quests, or whether these students have become Leaders, Followers, or Mogrifs, all of them have something to teach you about courage, persistence, and dedication to a cause bigger than oneself.

I am proud of every student who graduates from the School for Good and Evil—but I have a special place in my heart for this particular group of Evers and Nevers, the first to witness and survive a fairy tale that took place within these very walls. Imagine them not only having to attend classes, but also to contend with their own roles within a larger story, replete with war, suffering, and death.

In the end, they came out stronger for it, and so too will you, after hearing from them in the pages to come. For now you will know just how much we expect from each of you . . . and what big shoes you have to fill.

Sincerely,

Clarissa Dovey
Clarissa Dovey

Selected Portraits from the Graduating Class

EVERS

Tedros of Camelot

TRACK: Leader
QUEST: Restoring order, infrastructure, and financial stability to Camelot as its King

"Making difficult decisions in the face of adversity is what differentiates a boy from a man."
—Merlin of Ginnymill

Agatha of Woods Beyond

TRACK: Leader
QUEST: Reestablishing the role of the Queen of Camelot with an emphasis on social equality and civil rights

"You can enjoy jumping in puddles and still be a princess."
—Guinevere of Camelot

TRACK: Leader
QUEST: Defending Jaunt Jolie from rogue pirate fleets

"True beauty is in the eye of everyone with eyes."
—My mother

Beatrix of Jaunt Jolie

TRACK: Sidekick
QUEST: Organizing an army behind Beatrix to dispatch rogue pirate fleets in Jaunt Jolie

"You will never feel trapped as long as you have an imagination."
—Rapunzel of Roch Briar

Reena of Pasha Dunes

TRACK: Sidekick
QUEST: Tending the consecrated apple orchard atop Glass Mountain after last season's raging blight

"You never forget your first love . . . but you do learn to move on."
(RIP Tristan)
—Briar Rose of Maidenvale

Kiko of Neverland

TRACK: Sidekick
QUEST: Overseeing the knights of Camelot on King Tedros' behalf and developing the kingdom's new military strategy

*"Beware of green plants . . .
unless they've been ground up
in your morning smoothie."*
—Jack of Woods Beyond

Chaddick of Foxwood

TRACK: Mogrif (Raccoon)
QUEST: Delving into the treacherous lava-filled caves beneath the kingdom of Ravenbow to search for the Fountain of Youth

*"Even if your body
insists on growing up,
you can still act like a child."*
—Peter of Neverland (*aka Peter Pan*)

Tarquin of Rajashah

TRACK: Mogrif (Deer)
QUEST: Official lookout for Beatrix and Reena in the war against rogue pirates

"Sisters before misters."
—Ella of Maidenvale (*aka Cinderella*)

Millicent of Maidenvale

NEVERS

TRACK: Leader

QUEST: Serving as Dean and steering the School for Evil in a new direction, which it so *desperately* needed

"I'm happy on my own."
—ME

Sophie of Woods Beyond

TRACK: Leader

QUEST:

"True Evil means accepting Good as your equal."
—Lady Leonora Lesso

Hester of Ravenswood

Ravan of Thicket Tumble

TRACK: Leader
QUEST: Plundering the iron village of Akgul, where the last of the famous Akgul rubies are stored

"Urgh, garrrumph, whump."
—Gary the Great, Ogre Wrestling Champion of the Woods

TRACK: Henchman
QUEST: Supporting Dean Sophie's admirable mission to revitalize the School for Evil

"If at first you don't succeed in getting a lady to fall in love with you, you might as well just kill her."
—Drogan of Murmuring Mountains (aka Bluebeard)

Hort of Bloodbrook

Anadil of Bloodbrook

TRACK: Henchman
QUEST: **TOP SECRET**

"Every person becomes agreeable once you've removed his or her skeleton."
—the White Witch

Dot of Nottingham

TRACK: Henchman
QUEST:  TOP SECRET

"Life's too short. Eat whatever makes you happy."
—Gertrude of Knave's Peak
(*aka Hansel and Gretel's Witch*)

TRACK: Mogrif (Jellyfish)
QUEST: Kidnapping Missou, the fabled seer of Rainbow Gale, and forcing him to reveal prophecies about Evil's defeats so they can be prevented

"Always look up."
—Griselda of Ravenbow
(*aka the Wicked Witch of the East*)

Mona of Oz

Arachne of Foxwood

TRACK: Mogrif (Newt)
QUEST: Acting as a spy for Ravan in his quest to plunder the iron village of Akgul, where the last of the famous Akgul rubies are stored

"True villains don't quote other people."—Rabid Bear Rex

Superlatives BY HESTER

~~FAIREST~~ **Most Empty-Headed** OF THEM ALL
Beatrix

HANDSOMEST ~~OF THEM ALL~~ **Dunce of the Year**
Tedros

~~MOST GALLANT~~ **Best Ogre Bait**
Tedros

~~MOST REGAL~~ **Most Likely to Throw Her Life Away for a Blond Ninny** → **Most in Need of a Beating**
Tedros

~~MOST LIKELY TO SURVIVE THE ENDLESS WOODS~~
Agatha

~~BEST LEADERSHIP SKILLS~~ **Bossiest Loudmouth**
Sophie

MOST LIKELY TO ~~BEFRIEND~~ Get Eaten by
WOODLAND CREATURES
Reena

Loudest
Mouth-Breather
~~BIGGEST TRANSFORMATION~~
Hort

MOST VILLAINOUS^
Hester

and don't you
forget it

MOST SINISTER APPEARANCE
(close vote) Anadil

~~MOST LIKELY TO SWITCH SCHOOLS~~
Dot
Most
Traitorous

~~GENTLEST OF HEART~~
Most Likely to Kiko
Fall Down a Well

An Ever Never Roundtable

As soon as third year is over, 4 Evers and 4 Nevers are selected by the Deans to participate in a roundtable discussion, reflecting back on their time at school and searching for possible lessons that might help future students. For this roundtable, Dean Sophie nominated Hester, Anadil, Dot, and herself to participate from Evil, while Dean Dovey selected Chaddick, Kiko, Beatrix, and Reena to represent Good. A week before they embarked on their fourth-year quests, the chosen 8 gathered in the Clearing for tea, croissants, and lively conversation, transcribed in full by Albemarle.

SOPHIE: Welcome, welcome, my dear students! It is my honor to preside over this convocation of familiar faces and old friends—

HESTER: Okay, hold on. You may have been our Dean for our last year of school, but we were never your *students*. Nor are you *presiding*, because this is meant to be an honest discussion of our time at school, and to be "honest," none of us thinks of you as a Dean—we see you as one of *us*, a Nevergirl with a few cute party tricks and an ability to scheme and flirt your way to the top of Evil when, truth be told, you had no business being there. In fact, the only reason you're Dean at all is because Lady Lesso left you her dress, which, for

some reason, convinced senile old Dovey
that Lesso intended you to be Dean, when
I'm pretty sure Lesso just left you that
dress because you're the only girl on earth
who would wear purple by choice. And given
what you put us through as Dean during our
third year, I think the rules for today are
pretty simple: you speak only when we ask
you a question, and if you don't obey, we
break every single one of your limbs.

ANADIL: Oooh, I hope she speaks.

SOPHIE: Rude.

DOT: I actually think Sophie makes an excellent
Dean.

HORT: (*bursts in*) So do I.

(Everyone stares.)

HORT: (*looks at Sophie*) I thought you'd want me
here.

SOPHIE: Well, *now* I do. What were you and Dot
saying about me being an excellent Dean?

BEATRIX: Anyone who thinks you're an excellent
Dean has the brainpower of a potato. But
this has been my problem with Sophie since
day 1—everything's always about *her*. I
thought this was going to be a serious and
sober reflection on our time at school,
where each of us could say something
useful to the new class, and instead
we're talking about the Witch of Woods
Beyond . . . *again*.

SOPHIE: *Queen* of Woods Beyond, actually. I retain
my title even though Rafal's dead.

HESTER: Excuse me. What did I say?

SOPHIE: I will not be silent in the face of inaccuracy!

DOT: (*mouth full of croissant*) She makes a fair point.

ANADIL: (*gazing at Dot*) Dot, my dear, I wonder if your father ever considered trading you for a flank steak.

DOT: Um . . . how'd you know?

CHADDICK: Why don't we start by just talking about what happened after the War between Old and New? We should tell people what school was like during the rest of our third year.

BEATRIX: It was a lot like this . . . bickering uselessly amongst ourselves while Sophie redoes her lip gloss.

SOPHIE: I have to redo it every few hours, or my mouth will look dry and cracked like yours.

KIKO: The first month was rough: Nicholas' funeral, then taking shifts to help Merlin bury old heroes in the Garden of Good and Evil—

REENA: Plus we had to get used to being in separate schools again. We'd all helped to defend each other from the School Master, so there was a serious worry that we wouldn't be able to divide into Evers and Nevers again.

HESTER: Serious worry on *both* sides.

DOT: But that's where I think Dean Sophie did such a great job. She has this new vision for Evil that lets each of us be who we really are. During Lady Lesso's time as Dean, Evil relied on rejecting everything Good was about. But now Evil is about finding and expressing yourself, even if you're fat—

SOPHIE: At least *someone* gets it. (*pause*) Sort of.

HORT: Plus, we have better food, nicer-fitting clothes, and an Evil Groom Room with a full set of weights.

HESTER: This is why I hate boys. They're so easily bribed with low forms of entertainment.

DOT: Hester, you have to admit, some of the changes to the School for Evil have been for the better: the Points Challenge between Good and Evil, the chance to have a No Ball—

ANADIL: But that's just making us more like Good, isn't it? Everything Sophie's done to this school is just trying to turn this place into an Evil version of Good.

CHADDICK: I never thought of it that way. Deep.

HORT: If that's deep, I don't want to know what's shallow. In any case, Sophie's changes did prove that the system had been rigged all along, because Evil whomped Good so bad in the Ever-Never Challenge our third year—

BEATRIX: That's because we didn't have Agatha or Tedros on our team anymore! We lost our two top players—

DOT: Well, *we* didn't have Sophie on our team anymore—

REENA: Because she was too busy rigging the competition as your Dean!

SOPHIE: If you are accusing me of playing to Evil's strengths of courage and verve and exploiting Good's weaknesses, which are a direct result of them having a Dean who is addled and past her prime . . . well, then I am guilty in the first degree.

HESTER: Speaking of Agatha, did anyone actually ask her to be here?

CHADDICK: King Tedros and I exchanged a few letters. At first, he and Agatha sounded open to traveling from Camelot and joining in, but then Tedros said something came up. I also got the impression that he wasn't thrilled with the guest list for the roundtable . . . well, one person in particular.

(*Everyone looks at Sophie.*)

SOPHIE: He's a bit of a weenie, isn't he? Never thought a boy could be so easily intimidated.

CHADDICK: You're calling the King of Camelot a "boy"? I would like to remind you, your best friend is his queen—

SOPHIE: Not yet she isn't. They aren't married, which means she's not really anything, not even an official princess. And I don't see Tedros proposing to her in the near future. That boy isn't mature enough to take a bath by himself, let alone *marry* someone.

HORT: (*horrified*) You took a bath with him?

BEATRIX: WE'RE TALKING ABOUT SOPHIE *AGAIN*.

DOT: I have a question. While the rest of us went back to class, Tedros and Agatha had to leave for their quest early, since Tedros' coronation was coming up. Didn't everyone think school felt different with Tedros and Agatha gone?

SOPHIE: That's a terrible question. Ask something else.

KIKO: Um, I guess we could talk about Tracking. I mean, when the School Master was in charge, he'd started to turn me into a goose. I'm sure the new students will want to know how Tracking works now.

REENA: Once we all started attending classes again, it was clear that we'd still have to be tracked, so we could be divided up for our quests before fourth year. That's the way quests work: we're broken into teams made up of one Leader, a few Sidekicks, and a Mogrif or two. Each team is responsible for accomplishing a long-term assignment in the Endless Woods.

CHADDICK: And here's where Dovey came up with a smart solution, given our education at the school had been so haphazard—she postponed actual Mogrification until after the end of third-year classes, meaning those who were at risk of becoming animals and plants could actually get used to their new forms during their advanced courses. So if you were in the bottom third of the class and at risk of becoming a squirrel, you got to try out being that squirrel in Advanced Mogrification. . . . For some students, it made Mogrification less scary and even a little exciting. For others, it motivated them to raise their ranks over the course of third year and get out of that bottom group.

KIKO: Chaddick is so right. Once I was forced to live as a goose during my Mogrification seminar, I realized that it was all wrong

253

for me. I was destined to marry Tristan—if he hadn't died brutally at the hands of that ape Aric, of course—and Tristan would have been a Leader, for sure . . . so how could I have married him if I was a goose? Leaders don't marry *birds*! That motivated me to work extra hard and get my ranking points up, just enough to slip past the cutoff and end up as a sidekick. (*Tearing up*) Tristan would have been so proud of me.

HESTER: Amazing the stories we tell ourselves.

ANADIL: I think once we actually saw the stakes of Tracking, everyone worked harder. Well, except Brone, who appreciated being turned into a Stinkwood Tree, since it meant he didn't have to move anymore. Hey, Bea, how's Millicent doing, by the way?

BEATRIX: (*sighs*) She really did try to get her ranking up, poor thing—Reena and I helped her with her homework and studying for tests. . . . But she's a bit obtuse, as you know. I think she and Brone were the two lowest-ranked students in school.

REENA: They turned Millie into a deer. She was assigned to Beatrix's and my team—Bea is Leader, of course, and I am her sidekick. But when she heard we'd be fighting bloodthirsty pirates, Millie fled the school and went to Camelot, of all places. She'd found out that deer and stags are protected animals there, by Guinevere's order.

HESTER: Hmm . . . Ani, do you think we can get Agatha to revoke that protection?

ANADIL: I was thinking the same thing. . . .

SOPHIE: *(explodes)* You can't get Agatha to revoke anything, because Agatha isn't a queen! Agatha has no power! The only person who's officially a queen here is *me*!

(Silence)

DOT: Do you think they'll get married on the beach? Aggie and Teddy? Getting married on the beach is fashionable these days. Though I've tried turning sand into chocolate before and it still tastes briny—

SOPHIE: Dot, do you know if you hold your breath underwater for 15 minutes and pass out, you'll be woken up by a genie who grants you unlimited wishes?

DOT: Wouldn't you just drown and die?

SOPHIE: You'll have to try it and find out.

HORT: Should we talk about the Nevers' No Ball? It was pretty awesome. Our first real Evil dance—

SOPHIE: That's not true. We had one our first year—

ANADIL: That you *ruined* by barging in, warty and bald, and smashing things with an axe.

SOPHIE: Well, I made up for it this time, didn't I? Spared no expense. Live band, bonfire pit, body-painting stations . . .

HORT: It was awesome. Come on, Hester. Admit it.

HESTER: It was pretty intense. I'll give you that. Felt like we unleashed in this festival of smoke and fire and all turned into beasty little demons. Did I tell you, Ani, that at one point I realized my demon wasn't even

on my neck anymore? My tattoo jumped off
me so it could join the party.

ANADIL: Yeah, he bit me during a dance, because he
thought me and Ravan were getting too
close.

HESTER: Good boy. (*pats her twitching demon*)

ANADIL: What was with all the boys taking off their
shirts though?

HORT: Ummm, it was hot. And it's kind of what
boys do at a dance.

DOT: You and Sophie were cute together, by
the way. You kept snickering to each other
as the night went on and then I saw you
dancing to some fast-paced song before
Sophie put her arms around you, and this
was *after* you took your shirt off—

SOPHIE: (*throwing Dot a death glare*) *Excuse* me? I
did not dance with a shirtless Hort at the No
Ball, let alone have my arms around him. I
was too busy supervising as *Dean*!

HORT: Um, I'm pretty sure Dot's telling the truth.
Not just because I remember every time you
do anything to me, but also because you
whispered in my ear that we should—

SOPHIE: Let's talk about Agatha. I feel like we're
leaving her out.

DOT: But I tried to ask about Agatha before
and—

SOPHIE: Are you really still here?

BEATRIX: Much as I found her extremely overhyped,
I do think that Good is missing something
without Agatha. She was the one who made
us question what our classes truly meant.
During third year, Dovey and the faculty

invoked her all the time as an example of what a hero should be, but I'm not sure if that inspired us or discouraged us. Either way, without Agatha, it felt like all our levels dropped a bit—maybe that's why Good lost the Points Challenge so easily.

CHADDICK: Come on, it's not all bad. I mean, Tedros is freakin' King of Camelot now. Think of that. One of our own a King—and a Reader, his *queen*!

SOPHIE: PASS ME A CROISSANT.

DOT: But they have sugar, butter, wheat, and—

SOPHIE: I DON'T *CARE*.

DOT: (*whispers to Anadil*) Agatha and Tedros better not get married. If she's eating croissants now, what would happen at the actual *wedding*?

ANADIL: All I know is I better be invited.

HESTER: I'm sure the new kids will have questions about quests, as well. Not like we have a lot to tell them, since we just finished our third year and haven't even started our quests—

ANADIL: Wouldn't it have made sense to do this roundtable after the *fourth* year? Like, just before the new class is about to arrive? Doesn't it make sense to talk about our quests after we've actually *started* them?

SOPHIE: No, because some of you might die on your quests and then we'd have to find replacements, and Dovey and I have enough on our plates at the moment. Better to get this done before you leave. Plus, it takes time to print the handbooks. You know, full color and all.

CHADDICK: Oh God. Let's just take turns and talk about what we got assigned for our fourth-year quests.

BEATRIX: My homeland of Jaunt Jolie has been terrorized by pirates of late. We're a coastal kingdom, and every ship that tries to come in to deliver food or supplies gets attacked by filthy thugs. And it's not just one fleet of pirates—it's at least five or six. So I'm leading the team to fight them.

REENA: I'm one of Beatrix's sidekicks, along with Bastian, Flavia, and Oliver. Millicent was supposed to be our Mogrif, so now we're asking around to other teams to see if they've got one we can borrow since we'll need a lookout after we get to Jaunt Jolie.

CHADDICK: Bastian and Oliver are good enough fighters, I suppose, but how do you plan to beat five pirate ships all by yourselves?

BEATRIX: I don't. I plan to set them against each other and lead my team in to clean up the wreckage.

KIKO: Umm, how do you set five bands of pirates against each other?

BEATRIX: By making the leader of each band fall in love with me.

ANADIL: She's like a poor man's Sophie.

SOPHIE: So poor that it's hard to see the correlation.

BEATRIX: What's *your* quest, Anadil? Following your rats to Hamelin?

ANADIL: Hester, Dot, and I have a top secret

	quest we can't talk about, assigned by
	Dovey herself.
SOPHIE:	*Really*? I thought you were refurbishing
	Hester's gingerbread house into a new
	museum—
HESTER:	That's the quest you gave us. Dovey gave us
	a better one.
SOPHIE:	Dovey can't assign *Nevers* a quest! I
	demand to know what this unsanctioned
	mission is—
ANADIL:	And I demand your head on a platter.
	We all can't get what we want.
HESTER:	Besides, Dovey said explicitly not
	to tell you.
DOT:	She said if Sophie knew we were in
	charge of finding a new School Master,
	you'd—
SOPHIE:	*WHAT*?
DOT:	Oh no.

(*Chaddick lunges to stop Hester from throttling Dot.*)

HESTER:	You miserable, chocolate-sniffing worm!
DOT:	I'm not good with secrets! You know that!
SOPHIE:	I don't understand! How can there be a new
	School Master? Dovey and I are doing just
	fine as Deans without any supervision—
HESTER:	(*sighs*) Here's the situation. Professor
	Dovey thinks we need a new School Master
	who can protect the Storian. You may have
	started moving into the School Master's
	tower and turning it into your private
	headquarters, but that doesn't mean it's
	any more secure. The chance of the Storian

being stolen or corrupted is higher than ever. Besides, Dovey knows she's old and might die eventually, and no way is she leaving the selection of the next Dean of Good to *you*. So she had Yuba create a short list of candidates, and now Ani, Dot, and I are responsible for traveling to each candidate's kingdom and investigating them thoroughly in order to see whether they could make a suitable School Master.

SOPHIE: But if we have a new School Master, does that mean I'd have to move out of *my* tower?

ANADIL: *That's* what you're worried about?

SOPHIE: I don't want to work for anyone else! I like being my own boss! Suppose it's some ogreish, fusty woman, like . . . I don't know . . . *most* women!

KIKO: It could also be a boy who's super-cute and handsome.

SOPHIE: (*pauses*) I hadn't thought of that. Carry on questing, then.

HESTER: Hort, what's your quest?

HORT: Um . . . I've been asked to teach history at a local school.

KIKO: What school?

HORT: This one.

(*Everyone stares at him. They all laugh. Hort looks at Sophie, waiting for her to speak up. . . .*)

SOPHIE: Oh, what a lovely sunset. Look at how the purple comes off the clouds like a tidal wave—

BEATRIX:	Wait, Chaddick, what about you?
CHADDICK:	Tedros invited me to be his knight.
REENA:	You serious? Chaddick, that's amazing—
CHADDICK:	I'll be at his side as he brings in a whole new team to his Round Table. I have to pass the test first, of course.
HORT:	What kind of test?
CHADDICK:	Merlin will personally administer it in a few weeks, and apparently it's something you can't study for.
BEATRIX:	Whatever it is, I'm sure you'll pass it.
ESTER:	Even the Nevers won't disagree with that.
CHADDICK:	(*bright red*) Thanks, guys.
DOT:	That seems a nice note to end on, doesn't it?

(*Everyone starts standing up and dispersing as the sun sets.*)

SOPHIE:	Isn't anyone going to ask about my quest?

(*Kids leave.*)

SOPHIE:	Isn't anyone curious about my hopes and dreams?
HORT:	I am.

(*Sophie turns and sees he's the only one still there.*)

SOPHIE:	(*softly*) You don't think Lady Lesso left me this dress just because I look good in purple, do you?
HORT:	I think she made you Dean because you're

> brilliant, charismatic, hilarious, and the
> only person who she could ever imagine
> entrusting with the future of our school.

SOPHIE: (*blinking*) That . . . means a lot, Hort.

(*Sophie gets up, starts to leave.*)

> HORT: Can I ask you a question, too?

(*Sophie stops.*)

> You do remember dancing with me at the No
> Ball, don't you?

(*Sophie turns, smiling.*)

> SOPHIE: I even remember what I whispered in your
> ear.

(*Sophie leaves, but Hort stays there smiling and smiling
until he fades into the dark.*)

Admissions

The School for
Good and Evil
CAREER COUNSELING OFFICE

Dear New Students,

As much as your predecessors were a groundbreaking class
at the School for Good and Evil, you and your fellow Evers
and Nevers are also ushering in a new era for this institution.
Since its inception, the School for Good and Evil has evolved
in its process for selecting students. In the earliest years of the
school, for instance, the original School Master sent out howler
monkeys to recruit potential attendees. As the legend of the
school grew, however, subsequent School Masters had to modify
the admissions process in order to address the sheer volume of
applications received.

But with the recent death of our latest School Master, it seemed
an appropriate time to reevaluate the admissions process
once more. Rafal, after all, had single-handedly changed the
composition of our schools by importing Readers into the Endless
Woods. Unfortunately, his way of doing so not only lacked both
transparency and respect for Readers' personal safety, but also
limited the representation of Readers to only 2 per class.

Now, for the first time, applications at the School for Good and Evil will be equally open to both Readers and Descendants. Even though all of you have successfully completed this process in order to be part of our incoming class, we wanted to include our admissions materials in this Handbook so you can pass them along to friends and family members and also to help you understand why we accept and reject certain students.

Sincerely yours,

Marguerite Gasparyan

Marguerite Gasparyan
Admissions Director

Admissions Form
for Descendants

NAME:

ADDRESS:

EDUCATIONAL HIGHLIGHTS:

MENTORS (PLEASE SPECIFY IF MAGICAL):

LEGACY RELATIVE(S):

FAVORITE BOOK:

SPECIAL TALENTS OR ABILITIES:

IF YOUR HOUSE WERE BURNING DOWN, WHAT OR WHO WOULD YOU SAVE?

IF YOU WERE THROWING A PARTY, WHO WOULD YOU INVITE?

IF I WERE AN ANIMAL, I'D LIKE TO BE A:

REASONS FOR WANTING TO ATTEND THE SCHOOL FOR GOOD AND EVIL:

Admissions Form
for Readers

NAME:

ADDRESS:

EDUCATIONAL HIGHLIGHTS:

MOST ADMIRED PERSON:

FAVORITE BOOK:

IF I WERE AN ANIMAL, I'D LIKE TO BE A:

IF YOU WERE MAROONED ON A DESERTED ISLAND,
WHAT 3 THINGS WOULD YOU WANT TO HAVE?

REASONS FOR WANTING TO ATTEND THE SCHOOL FOR GOOD AND EVIL:

Admissions Form for Descendants

NAME:
Delia of Maidenvale

ADDRESS:
Delia
The Biggest House in the Neighborhood at—
108 Juniper Avenue
Maidenvale

EDUCATIONAL HIGHLIGHTS:
♡ Busiest Beaver and Best Smile Awards
from my tutor, Madame Hibou
♡ Taught humility and fashion sense
to all by being the richest and best dressed

MENTORS (PLEASE SPECIFY IF MAGICAL):
Madame Hibou and Maman agree that I am the perfect
mentor for myself. And I am rather magical.

LEGACY RELATIVE(S):
My uncle King Alphonse, formerly known as the
Marquis of Carabas. He starred in his own fairy tale, but
for some reason people only remember his dumb cat who
wore boots.

FAVORITE BOOK:
Last year I wrote a novel that made everyone cry, including me. That's my favorite.

SPECIAL TALENTS OR ABILITIES:
A better question would be, which talents _don't_ I have? But drawing, singing, dancing, acting, and shopping are my best.

IF YOUR HOUSE WERE BURNING DOWN, WHAT OR WHO WOULD YOU SAVE?
It would never burn down! I read a book on emergency house rescue once, so I'm pretty sure I'd be able to put out a fire, no matter the size, without losing a single belonging.

IF YOU WERE THROWING A PARTY, WHO WOULD YOU INVITE?
I know soooo many people, so the truth is, I'd open it to everyone so no one would think I was playing favorites. Because I practically do know _everyone_.

IF I WERE AN ANIMAL, I'D LIKE TO BE A:
Butterfly, but only if I can change the color of my wings whenever I want.

REASONS FOR WANTING TO ATTEND THE SCHOOL FOR GOOD AND EVIL:
I am more than qualified, and it is my destiny to star in my own fairy tale someday.

REJECTED

ADMISSIONS NOTES

While I have no doubt that Delia is committed to achieving excellence in every aspect of her life, I gather from her responses that she feels as though she has already learned everything she needs to know. We expect our incoming Evers and Nevers to be like sponges, ready to soak up all that their new environment has to offer. My concern with Delia is that her arrogance will preclude her from truly achieving her potential at school.

—DEAN DOVEY

Admissions Form for Descendants

NAME:
Jolof of Kingdom Kyrgios

ADDRESS:
Jolof
825 Kidney Bean Street
Hot Stew Circle
Kingdom Kyrgios

EDUCATIONAL HIGHLIGHTS:
✳ Stayed awake during a full lecture
✳ Built a pile of walnut shells on my desk
✳ Watched an ant walk from one side of the classroom to the other without blinking
✳ Learned how to raise both eyebrows at the same time

MENTORS (PLEASE SPECIFY IF MAGICAL):
I don't like the noises in my house, and my shadow has been very comforting and protective.

LEGACY RELATIVE(S):
My great-aunt Phyllis was a Mofrig. Or is it griffom? Either way, she went to the School for Good and Evil and then got to live the rest of her life as a sloth, with unlimited naps.

FAVORITE BOOK:
My pillow

SPECIAL TALENTS OR ABILITIES:
I can almost fit in a barrel.

IF YOUR HOUSE WERE BURNING DOWN, WHAT OR WHO WOULD YOU SAVE?
My barrel

IF YOU WERE THROWING A PARTY, WHO WOULD YOU INVITE?
I don't know that many people, but I would want someone to bring food, someone to bring drinks, someone to bring ice . . . oh, and someone to send out the invitations.

IF I WERE AN ANIMAL, I'D LIKE TO BE A:
Earthworm, so I can burrow into a hole in the ground at the first sign of trouble.

REASONS FOR WANTING TO ATTEND THE SCHOOL FOR GOOD AND EVIL:
It sounds easy, plus, I've been asked not to return to the school in my town.

REJECTED

ADMISSIONS NOTES

While the applicant has a few traits commonly associated with the School for Good (a love of comfort and an appreciation of sufficient rest), for the most part, I have a hard time believing that this person is willing to fight for any cause, Good or Evil.

—PRINCESS UMA

Admissions Form for Readers

ADMISSIONS DIRECTOR'S NOTE: Admission or Rejection isn't always so cut and dried! Have a look at one of our thornier cases . . .

NAME:	ADDRESS:
Nicola of Woods Beyond	Nicola (Ask for "Nic")
[Submitted by her friend Hunter because no way is she applying on her own]	21 Honeycomb Circle
	Gavaldon

EDUCATIONAL HIGHLIGHTS:
- Founder of the Gavaldon unisex rugby team
- Currently campaigning for the girls' uniforms to include pants instead of skirts

MOST ADMIRED PERSON:
She admires any girl who challenges a boy to a fight and wins.

FAVORITE BOOK:
A Girl's Guide to Survival in a Man's World

IF I WERE AN ANIMAL, I'D LIKE TO BE A:
A bonobo, because the males of the species are submissive to the females.

IF YOU WERE MAROONED ON A DESERTED ISLAND, WHAT 3 THINGS WOULD YOU WANT TO HAVE?
1) A soccer ball
2) A hockey stick
3) A set of dumbbells (and none of this 5-lb. nonsense)

REASONS FOR WANTING TO ATTEND THE SCHOOL FOR GOOD AND EVIL:
Because there's a greater place for her in the world where she can learn a girl's true worth, and I don't think it's here.

ADMISSIONS NOTES
Dear Deans Dovey & Sophie—I found this message in our files recently and believe it pertains to this very student . . . ?

ᐳFROM THE OFFICE OF AUGUST E. SADERᐸ

A word to our future Deans:
In a class to come, you will encounter a prospective student named Nicola of Woods Beyond. You will see no immediate reason to accept her. But I request that you override your misgivings. As usual, I cannot answer any questions as to why, not only because seers cannot answer questions, but also because I will be long dead by the time you discover this note. But I will say this: her acceptance to our school will play a crucial role in its future survival.

A.E.S.

Dean Dovey: I don't want her.

Dean Sophie: I don't want her either.

Dean Dovey: Shall we flip a coin?

Dean Sophie: Come to my office and I'll do it.

Dean Dovey: It'll be done by a neutral observer with witnesses to verify an honest result.

Dean Sophie: FINE.

ACCEPTED
SCHOOL FOR EVIL

MY TALENT ◇ Costume Design
by Loris of Bremen

Peacock

Ladder

Puddle

A YEAR OF EVIL DEEDS
by Gordon of Walleye Spring

January 1—Teased a wasp

January 2—Put porcupine needles in Mum's tea

January 3—Burned my sister's love letters

January 4—Trimmed teacher's hair when her back
was turned

January 5—Stuffed toenails into Mum's cherry pie

IN PRAISE OF MISSING TEETH

by QUINKITA OF NUPUR LALA

When I was a child
My teeth shimmered like spun gold
But I felt that my shining smile
Clashed with my darkened soul.

I tried to dye my hair
I tried to change my clothes
But despite my grandest efforts
I looked sweeter than a rose.

Then one day a girl in class
Tried to take my lunch
It made me very angry
So I threw a heavy punch.

She hit me back quite hard
Right below the lip
I felt the pain course through my mouth
And my stomach began to flip.

Now without my two front teeth
I am finally myself
They're better off sitting
In a bottle on my shelf.

A Day with Me and My Friends

By Papusa of Nettle Forest

QUICK AND EASY WAYS TO BRIGHTEN YOUR LIFE

by RUBY of WOODS BEYOND

1) Sprinkle edible gold leaf in your oats to infuse the morning with some extra shimmer.

2) Serve sapphire-infused sugar cubes at your next tea party.

3) Place a tiny diamond or crystal on the end of each of your eyelashes to add flash to every flirtatious wink.

4) Hire a dove to shower the audience with glitter during your next harp performance.

5) Two words (for old people only): platinum dentures

The School for
Good and Evil

FAQ
(Frequently Asked Questions)

Dear Evers and Nevers,

In reading your applications, essays, and letters, we've noticed a number of common questions that you've had not only about the School for Good and Evil, but also about events concerning our most recent graduating class. Rather than allow myth and misinformation to perpetuate, we have chosen to address these questions head-on so that you may have the clearest view of our school as you prepare to begin your first year. To that end, each query has been answered by an alumnus or faculty member who we believed was best equipped to address a given situation.

Sincerely,

Marguerite Gasparyan

Marguerite Gasparyan
Admissions Director

1. WHAT WAS THE NAME OF RAFAL'S BROTHER?

Professor August Sader alludes to this on page 220 of A *Student's Revised History of the Woods*:

"Neither of the proper names of the Good School Master or the Evil School Master was ever known, though in my own dealings with the latter, I can attest to hearing the Evil School Master—now known as Rafal—casually refer to his own brother as 'Rhian.' Whether that was indeed the Good brother's name or merely a slip of the tongue, we'll never know."

---

2. HOW OLD ARE SOPHIE AND AGATHA?

DEAN SOPHIE: Old enough to know that this is a terrifically *rude* question.

---

3. WHO WAS ARIC'S FATHER?

PROFESSOR DOVEY: Lady Lesso never spoke of Aric's father to me, but I do remember a hulking, well-muscled man coming to the castle gates about ten years ago, asking if Leonora was in. He had the darkest eyes, filled with a fiery madness, and even standing in his presence for just a few moments, I sensed danger. When I found Leonora and described him to her, she went white as milk—she begged me to go back to the man and tell him that she'd deserted the school long before and to ensure that the man never came searching for her at the schools again. I did as she asked, but when I later tried to press Leonora on who this man was, she turned cold and made it clear that it was none of my business. When I met Aric years later, however, I realized that the man who came to the gates that day must have been his father. A man who is surely still alive, somewhere in the Endless Woods.

---

4. **WHY WAS THERE A FUNERAL HELD ONLY FOR CINDERELLA AND LADY LESSO BUT NONE FOR THE OTHER STUDENTS AND CREATURES WHO FOUGHT IN THE OLD-NEW WAR?**

PROFESSOR DOVEY: I do lament that *The Tale of Sophie and Agatha* suggests that we only held funerals for Cinderella and Lady Lesso after the end of the war. We had a proper burial for Nicholas the next evening, as well as burials for all those who'd died at the hands of Rafal and his zombie army, supervised by Merlin in the Garden of Good and Evil. This long-term burial effort continues, which will hopefully be accelerated once a new Crypt Keeper is appointed to tend to the Garden.

5. **ON THE STORIAN, THERE ARE SOME WEIRD ENGRAVINGS—DO THEY MEAN ANYTHING OR SAY ANYTHING SPECIAL?**

PROFESSOR DOVEY: Students asked this question of Professor August Sader every year, and his answer was the same: "The answer will come to light in its own time. Perhaps in another fairy tale, soon to be written."

6. **HOW IS JACK ALIVE IN *THE TALE OF SOPHIE AND AGATHA* WHEN HE WAS KIDNAPPED 100 YEARS AGO?**

YUBA: Jack, like many successful fairy-tale heroes, learned the art of life extension, which most witches in the Endless Woods are willing to teach, if an Ever can pay enough gold. Given his plunder of the Giant's kingdom, Jack ensured he'd live well beyond the years of an ordinary mortal.

7. **WERE THE STORIES REWRITTEN DURING THE OLD-NEW WAR RETURNED TO THEIR ORIGINAL STATE ONCE GOOD TRIUMPHED?**

MERLIN: Though the old heroes could not be revived, their

Ever Afters were restored upon Rafal's death and will remain untouched and untampered with for the rest of time. Or at least, we hope.

---

8. WILL SOPHIE FIND LOVE?

SOPHIE: Goodness, don't worry about me. I'll find love when it's time. But right now, I'm enjoying the calm and peace of knowing that I'm happy on my own. Plus, my workload as Dean is as intense as it is never ending! But I do appreciate your concerns. Just know that every Ever After is unique to the person, just as yours will be unique to you. (Besides, now that my fairy tale has come out all around the Woods, I'm *famous*. And fame is a rather compelling substitute for love.)

---

9. DO AGATHA AND TEDROS HAVE ANY KIDS?

We received a couriered message from Tedros in response to this question:

"DO I SEEM LIKE SOMEONE WHO'S READY FOR KIDS ANYTIME SOON?"

---

10. WHEN SOPHIE TOOK RAFAL'S RING, WERE THEY TECHNICALLY MARRIED?

SOPHIE: Taking Rafal's ring was a deep act of commitment between the two of us. Had he lived, I'm sure we would have been married one day. (Though I wonder what I would have worn—who wants to see a bride in *black*?)

---

11. WHO LOOKS AFTER THE STORIAN NOW?

PROFESSOR DOVEY: The Storian remains in the School Master's old tower, temporarily —and illicitly—converted into Dean Sophie's private headquarters, until a better arrangement is found. In the meantime, Dean Sophie is technically responsible for protecting the Storian, though Good has a full fleet of new fairies supervising the tower at all times.

12. **HOW DOES THE SCHOOL MASTER DECIDE WHO BECOMES AN EVER AND WHO BECOMES A NEVER?**
YUBA: That is the hallmark of a true School Master—the ability to look into each of our souls and to see the kernel of truth from which all things bloom, whether it is Good or Evil. Until a new School Master is appointed, however, the Deans are responsible for selecting new students who best fit into their schools.

⎯⎯⎯⎯

13. **WAS NEVERLAND FOUNDED BY NEVERS?**
HORT: Oooh. Sounds like you figured it out! Yes, and one day someone will write the *real* story that tells the truth about Peter Pan and his Lost Boys. Neverland was raided by Evers and claimed for Good, even though they had no rights to the kingdom whatsoever. That's why I fight so hard to protect my father's legacy—in my eyes, Captain Hook was the real hero; and Peter Pan, Wendy, and all Peter's other stooges were lawless, pillaging invaders.

⎯⎯⎯⎯

14. **IF A READER FROM GAVALDON IS KIDNAPPED EVERY FOUR YEARS, WHY DOES *THE TALE OF SOPHIE AND AGATHA* ONLY UNFOLD OVER THREE YEARS AT SCHOOL?**
CASTOR: AIN'T YOU BEEN READING? FOURTH YEAR IS WHEN KIDS GO ON QUESTS OUTSIDE OF SCHOOL AND TRY NOT TO DIE, BUT IF THEY DIE WE SAY A QUICK PRAYER FOR 'EM LIKE WE DID FOR BEEZLE AND THEN GO BACK TO EATING BACON.

⎯⎯⎯⎯

15. **HOW DO YOU BECOME A TEACHER AT THE SCHOOL FOR GOOD AND EVIL?**
PROFESSOR DOVEY: Whenever a position opens, the respective Deans of each school are responsible for finding a qualified faculty member who will move into the castle and

not be encumbered by their former life outside of it. Each faculty appointment is intended to be a lifetime appointment. (As for Hort's nomination as history professor, let's just say that was a case of being in the right place at the right time.)

---

16. WHERE DO VILLAINS GO TO THE BATHROOM?

ANADIL: If you don't know, you're not a real villain.

---

17. WHAT HAPPENED TO ALL THE EVERS AFTER THEY WENT BACK TO SCHOOL AFTER THE END OF THE GOOD-EVIL WAR? WERE THEIR TRACKING SCORES CHANGED, OR DID THEY KEEP THEM EVEN THOUGH THEIR SCORES REFLECTED RAFAL'S EVIL CURRICULUM? (BECAUSE IT SEEMS UNJUST THAT KIKO WOULD HAVE TO MOGRIFY FOR FAILING EVIL WHEN SHE'S CLEARLY GOOD!)

PROFESSOR DOVEY: As mentioned in the graduates' roundtable, I was aware of this injustice and granted students a full year of study before tracks were assigned to ensure they could raise their rankings and avoid Mogrification (if they *wanted* to, that is; a number of students came to embrace their new animal forms and welcomed being in the bottom of the group).

---

18. SINCE THERE'S ONLY ONE STORIAN, ONLY ONE STORY CAN BE WRITTEN AT A TIME. WHAT HAPPENS IF TWO OR MORE INTERESTING THINGS ARE HAPPENING AT ONCE? DOES THE PEN HAVE TO PICK WHICH IS MORE INTERESTING, OR DOES IT WRITE ONE AFTER IT HAPPENED?

YUBA: That is the supreme power of the Storian: to look at all things happening in all the world and to know the right story to tell at the right time.

Dear Students,

From dining to history to class descriptions, we've given you a thorough introduction to the school that will be your home for the next three years. That said, if you have any further questions about the School for Good and Evil, your Deans or your teachers can surely answer them. We hope the Ever Never Handbook has provided you with all you need to be successful as you begin your education here. Most important, we hope it has given you the confidence and determination to find your Ever or Never After, like so many others have before.

Best of luck and see you in the halls!

Clarissa Dovey
Dean Sophie

Hester
18 Rotten Peach Lane
(Gingerbread House)
Ravenswood

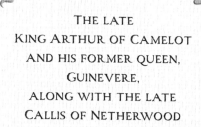

THE LATE
KING ARTHUR OF CAMELOT
AND HIS FORMER QUEEN,
GUINEVERE,
ALONG WITH THE LATE
CALLIS OF NETHERWOOD

REQUEST THE HONOR OF YOUR PRESENCE
AT THE WEDDING OF THEIR CHILDREN

King Tedros of Camelot

TO

Agatha of Woods Beyond

ON

THE 14TH OF OCTOBER
AT HALF PAST TWO

CASTLE GROUNDS
CAMELOT

STUDENT NOTES

STUDENT NOTES

STUDENT NOTES

STUDENT NOTES

STUDENT NOTES

STUDENT NOTES

Calling All Readers!

Dear Readers,

For the first time in our history, we are now accepting applications from <u>you</u> to attend our prestigious school!

Think you have what it takes? Below is a list of required reading for every applicant. You MUST finish it if you hope to apply successfully, although acing a fashion challenge or a light torture test will also put you miles ahead.*

(*Prof. Dovey's note: This is the Dean of Evil's idea of "humor." Please simply complete the reading.)

Signed,
Clarissa Dovey & Sophie of Woods Beyond